# NAMESTONE

Past meets present in a fight to possess the cosmos

Anthony Shephard

*Tony Shephard*

## instant apostle

*anthonyjinuk.com*

First published in Great Britain in 2015.

Instant Apostle
The Barn
1 Watford House Lane
Watford
Herts
WD17 1BJ

British Library Cataloguing-in-Publication Data

A catalogue record for this book is available from the British Library

This book and all other Instant Apostle books are available from Instant Apostle:

Website: www.instantapostle.com

E-mail: info@instantapostle.com

ISBN 978-1-909728-27-1

Printed in Great Britain

To my wife Audrey, to whose love and understanding
I owe more than words can say.

# Prologue

Stars burn in an infinity of black.

The black itself burns with an intensity that would be painful to the eyes, but there is no observer; or perhaps just one. The whole creation is a vast, stretched harmony. What words are there for its state? Active yet poised; tense yet free; in its totality like a solid and like a fluid; void yet pregnant, intense, personal. What could an 'outside' observer see? There is, after all, no outside from which it can be seen. The whole pregnant mass, if there were an outside, would take smooth glistening form – but form of what?

'See! I hold it in my hand. What do you see?

'You see a stone? But what stone is like this stone?

'Look at it. Do not look at me. You could not survive that – not yet.

'Look. Listen. Feel.

'Here is life. Here is the pulse of all things.

'Watch.'

Like a single heartbeat the universe pulses, beats, and is never the same again.

Not because it is changed.

But because you are.

# 1

## Simon Verderer, July 1573

The tree grew vertically from a shallow incline at the edge of a small clearing. The directional cut was set for a fall straight down the slope towards the new trackway prepared for its removal. Sunlight filtered through the canopy and a dapple of light moved on the forest floor. Five of them had worked steadily in the bright shade – Simon Verderer, Eduard his bailiff with his two men Iuan and Giles, and David, Giles' younger son. Now Iuan and Giles plied the axes for the final blows while Simon and Eduard watched from a respectable distance with young David. Below on the trackway other workers waited with the ox cart.

Simon was uneasy.

As axe blow followed axe blow, Simon looked up into the arched canopy above, where sunlight shone green through the upper leaves, watching for the first sign of movement, the earliest beginnings of the tree's fall. He looked down past the axemen at the lie of the slope, the placing of the directional cut and the steadily enlarging felling cut. All was well set for a perfect lie.

In his mind's eye he saw it as he had from horseback earlier that week. The animal had resisted his urging for a few moments at the crest but then they had come down easily and he had turned, looking up at the tree he had chosen. Why should he think of that now? And why that strange sensation, a reluctance like his horse at the slope's brow, hesitating by the trunk of the oak, a Goliath to be felled.

He looked up again and felt rather than saw the first movement of the mass above him.

'Stop! Get back! Giles! Iuan!'

He found himself shouting urgent commands. What had got into him? The men backed away. He looked again at the crest of the slope where the horse had hesitated and saw it move. At once he looked at the felling cut, saw it close and listened for the explosion of sound that would signal the fall. It came strangely muffled, and the tree hung. The movement in the ground stopped for no more than a moment, and he looked again at the canopy above and was astonished to see it still moving. The sense of feeling it move returned in the faintest of tremors under his feet. In that instant the ground at the root of the great tree heaved and the whole trunk began to move again, tearing its roots with it. The slope was soft or unstable and the roots gave way before the cut.

David gave a boyish shriek of delight and danced forwards, but Simon was quick to seize his shoulder and draw him back. A shower of snapping roots and soil broke from the earth, the new slender ones cutting up from the earth like cheese wires until one by one they snapped. The final one parted, springing back like a whip. Simon was lashed by a stinging hail of earth and gravel. David at his side fell back on the grass. As the tree hit the slope the cut finally parted under the shock, and the trunk jumped a little way from the root and was still.

A small shower of leaves drifted around them like an autumn fall. They stood gazing at the sight for a moment and then Simon looked down at the boy. He was unnaturally still. A dark smear of earth on his forehead had the worrying appearance of a misshapen bruise. Simon knelt beside him as the others gathered round. The boy was limp and white. His father knelt at his other side and patted his cheeks to revive him, but to no avail.

There was no blood, but his forehead had darkened ominously where he had been hit by a flying stone; it was soft and irregular to the touch. Try as they might, they could find no sign of life.

They bore him to Greenway, a sad, pitiful bundle in his father's arms, and thence to his own home. Simon and Eduard remained at the home a while after the others had left, then left themselves as the priest arrived.

# 2

Greenway was a small English midlands manor set in rolling hills, bearing a somewhat neglected air. It was neither wealthy nor poor, but its servants were well treated. Their master, Simon Verderer, shared in the work on an equal but understood basis. The few tenant farmers in the outlying region were no more dilatory in their rents than most, and collection rarely had to be enforced.

Unusually for those turbulent late Tudor times, the estates ran themselves well. The soil was fertile and maintenance had been made easier by the diligence of a succession of conscientious masters, of which Simon was the last in a line that stretched back almost five hundred years. The lands were greater then, the times harder, and a more repressive regime was the day's order, but since Henry's day the land was more settled. As long as a man applied himself to his labours and his lands, did not dabble in the turmoil of the religious disputes that had bedevilled Mary's reign, and kept himself no more and no less god-fearing than he needed to be, then tolerable living could be wrung from the land.

Life could be pleasant in the summer and was survivable in the winter. The past fifteen years of Elizabeth's reign had not changed that. Indeed, things were in many ways much improved. But for all that, the manor had a diminished air. Not that Simon was a weak master – no estate could survive that – he ruled firmly and gained the respect of his men and women by rising early, toiling solidly alongside them when the work demanded, and supervising his own and his tenants' lands with a practised eye. Why, then, the neglected air? The hedging and ditching was attentive and regular, crops did not rot for lack of drainage nor animals wilt for lack of shade. There was a degree of untidiness, certainly, which extended more to the manor than to the farmland. The roof was sound and the walls and doors secure, but an observer might notice that a job once done remained just that – complete but not completed; the leavings of labour, surplus tiles, wood shavings and nails were not cleared away. Observant as the master was of what needed to be done, he appeared not to notice any traces left afterwards.

It was generally considered that the manor lacked a mistress. Talk in the evenings was mainly contented but frequently underlaid with concern. Simon for his part seemed genuinely at ease with his state and rarely ventured from his lands, and certainly not in search of a wife, but there was a sense among the workers and their wives of something missing. A house needed a mistress, and Simon was the last in a line.

'He should hunt … get about more. He visits no one and no one visits us!'

'Stop fretting, woman. The house runs well, doesn't it?'

'You'd not notice if it fell into the cellars! He never meets anyone. He should live more while he's still young. Where are the sons who will carry the line?'

'You and I will be gone long before then!'

'So that is alright is it? The devil take it when we're gone!'

Samuel frowned disapproval at his wife's language, but they knew each other too well for it to mean much between them. Aging retainers as they were, there was truth in what he said; they had both invested long lives in Greenway, as their fathers had before them.

'There's time yet.'

Time is a variable commodity in the human mind; it runs at different speeds on different trackways. It eats up the endless boredom of wasted hours in minutes, so we wonder where the time is gone that had seemed to drag so slowly. We notice the minutes and miss the years. Simon Verderer was still a young man by present standards, but in the sixteenth century life was shorter and prone to change in an instant. His retainers were right to be concerned; change would be welcome and timely.

Simon was making one of his regular rounds of his tenants' farms. A few weeks before each quarter day he would set aside one week, each day of which he would mount his horse and set off in one seemingly random direction or another with his bailiff and the two men. There was deliberation in this. He did not want his tenants to spot a routine that they might anticipate; far better that they should receive him unannounced and unexpected.

It was early one September morning, heavy with the dews that presaged the coming of autumn. Leaves were already curling red at their edges and the berries ripening in the hedges. The horses' hooves kicked up a mist of spray which caught the early sun, and the four rode with a sense of contentment. But there was a heaviness to it. The death of Giles's son David two months before still weighed on master and man. Giles kept to his own thoughts; he held no blame to his master. No one could have foreseen what had happened. If he blamed anyone he blamed himself. He was a woodsman; his master was not. But Simon did lay blame. The death of David by a slingshot from a giant had preyed on his mind as a blasphemy God should not have allowed. Nevertheless, the rising sun in the September mist gave a sense of newness, a salve to sadness.

It was well beyond first light when they rode into Spey with the warm sun on the settlement rooftops raising a vapour from the eastward thatch. The bustle of the farmyard focused on them, and moments later Thomas Gerard came out to greet them. The horses were taken to be rubbed down and the men took their ease while Simon and bailiff Eduard went inside with Thomas.

They had breakfasted and almost completed their business when a clatter of hooves outside betrayed the presence of another arrival. Thomas went out to the farmyard, and Simon and Eduard followed.

Four men accompanied two luggage horses and two palfreys. One of the palfreys carried a plump female, past middle age, who fussed like a nanny over the dark-haired, finely but simply dressed young woman who sat quietly on the other. Her mistress wore a simple linen tunic over finer skirts and sleeves showing black beneath. Instead of a wimple she wore a French cap, black to match her silk sleeves in which slashes shone deep orange.

Simon, having been the first to enter the farmhouse, had been the last to leave, and stood admiring this vision before him. He had no need to speak but felt for the moment tongue-tied, gladly letting Thomas make the usual enquiries.

'The Lady Davina Maerham.'

The words filtered into his brain with what seemed an infinite slowness, as if they had travelled from the stars. But the name 'Davina' fell on his ears with an unwonted heaviness. Momentarily he saw again the small boy David lying dead at his feet, slain by Goliath with a slingshot.

As someone helped her dismount he saw tiredness in her face mixed with some other care, like a shadow. All was not well with her, and he fought an irritation at the unfairness of a world in which death and care ignored hopes and expectations.

He had not realised until that moment how much young David's death troubled him. Why should he feel this now? Was it just the similarity in the names, or the sight of unknown sorrow on a beautiful stranger's face coupled with her mourning dress?

'My lady is bound for Marylesse,' the lady in attendance said bluntly. 'We had lodging at Riseholme and set on early to be there well before evening, but my lady's pony is lame with a swollen fetlock, and to press it further might give us problems on the way.'

He would have returned to the house, leaving Thomas Gerard to make arrangements, but catching his movement Lady Maerham looked directly at him, and he felt obliged to acknowledge her.

'Simon Verderer, Master of Greenway and the holdings hereabouts, at your service, my lady.'

She nodded. 'May I crave a boon, my lord? I fear my horse being lame will not complete our journey. I shall use one of the palfreys but if this beast could be attended to by your people, Elian here would redeem her and pay for her keep on his return.'

'I would not see you inconvenienced one jot, Lady Maerham. My own mount, I fear, is rather high and skittish for you, but my bailiff's man Iuan rides a smaller mare, and I am sure Master Thomas would furnish him with a suitable mount until your return.'

'Your offer is kindly meant and gladly accepted. I will not be returning but Elian will pass by in two days to make the exchange and make good any outstanding debt.'

'There will be no debt, my lady, but will you not return? Have you kin in Marylesse? It is a far journey.'

Her response was a light nod.

After a pause, perhaps because of a sense of being too dismissive, she said simply, 'I have family obligations there long neglected which I can now fulfil. Perhaps Master Thomas could provide some refreshment while the horses are attended to?'

Thomas called his wife who ushered lady and maid inside while the men saw to the horses. With trampled straw steaming under their feet, one of the stablemen transferred Lady Davina's saddle to the fresh mare and sent a lad to the kitchen for a mallow poultice for the injured animal. Simon watched on with his mind elsewhere, his eyes following the boy's progress across the sunlit yard.

Thomas looked at Elian. 'Does your mistress travel far from her manor and her lord to her family? We do not know her here.'

Like his lady's, Elian's reply was brief. 'Lady Maerham is widowed these eight months. Her decisions are her own.' He was not prepared to be drawn further.

Simon left Thomas to his charge and turned towards the house. At the last moment he turned away and walked beyond to the kitchen garden. Pausing to survey the neat rows of vegetables, he kicked his toe idly into the well-turned soil then, with a grunt of irritation for which he could have given no reason, he returned to the house.

## Frank Scanlon, July 2008

*He folded the letter slowly and fed it into the shredder. That might be a mistake, but if he needed the details again he only had to ask. In the meantime he would take some time off. The lab was running smoothly and nothing needed his personal attention. Besides, he was overdue some leave. He felt a sudden longing for fresh air and hills, and the feel of wind or rain on his face.*

## 1573

The ten riders set out with the two palfreys as far as the track to Greenway where Simon sent the bailiff and the two men on while he stayed with Davina's party.

'If you will grant me the boon of giving some small service, I shall be pleased to accompany you to the limit of my holdings. The way is not direct and I shall be pleased to set you on your way.'

After a short pause Davina gave a small smile. 'Your offer is kind, as was that of this mare. It would be churlish of me to accept the one and not the other.'

As he rode alongside her, the thought of David came strongly back to him. He had removed a dried leaf from the tree from the boy's tunic, and at the short, sad funeral he had picked another from the ground and crumpled its remains over the small coffin.

There was no similarity other than name between this beautiful, self-possessed young widow and Giles' boy, but seeing her seated on Iuan's mare he felt the same unease that he had felt at the tree's felling. He thrust the morbidity contemptuously aside but found light conversation difficult – not altogether because of these thoughts: Davina was disturbing for other, far more delightful reasons.

'I trust you will find your family well, my lady,' he said at length, 'but am grieved that you will not be returning. I would much like to entertain you at Greenway.'

'Another season, my lord, perhaps you may.'

They rode on, her maid a little to the rear and her men ahead. Later, Simon could remember nothing of their conversation, but he returned captivated, stopping occasionally to turn his horse and look back.

## *August 2008*

*Scanlon adjusted his backpack and headed west. He had watched the dawn from the train window and alighted into a cold but welcoming sunlight. About twenty minutes later he was in open country following a stone-walled lane towards a village whose name he did not know. He had no map. This was a deliberate decision: he did not want to know either his terrain or his destination. This was to be a walking holiday with a distinct difference; comfort and security were the last things on his mind.*

# 3

## Late September 1573

After two weeks there had been neither word from Thomas nor return of the mare, but it was a busy time and spare hands were few. At the end of the third week Simon had begun to wonder, when a disturbance in the courtyard drew him outside. The mare was standing by the barns, cornered by two stable boys who seemed reluctant to approach closer.

'She's wild, sir. Take care. She bit at Will here when he went near her.'

Simon approached her slowly. She was scratched and dirty with dried blood on her withers, and she eyed him with her head up, dancing from side to side with her front feet. He took slow steps forwards, murmuring softly. Slowly her head lowered and the dancing steps stopped.

Iuan's voice spoke quietly from behind him. 'There, Tess, there now, come, come.'

Bit by bit the mare quietened and the two men took her by the bridle. She was in a sorry state: wounds caked with blood and dirt were scattered over her legs, and her rump carried a deeper, disrupted wound where something had entered the flesh and torn its way out again. Iuan inspected it with concern. 'If you ask me, sir, that's an arrow mark. Yes, for sure, you can see where it pierced sharp going in and tore the skin on its way out. Maybe she tore it off in a bush herself.'

Filled with concern, Simon assembled a party of men while they sent the mare to be washed and treated. Within the hour they were riding to Spey. Before the Marylesse turn, Simon gave instructions for the party to split. Some would go to Spey to give and enquire of news, and to raise more for a search party, while the rest would make on to Marylesse. His plans, however, proved all too unnecessary.

As they approached the turn, two riders came from Spey with the worst of news. A monk from the hermit-like monastery of St Antipas-in-Pergamon had been found some way from the ride to Marylesse and brought in a few days before. An arrow in his chest had pierced a lung. In spite of the aid they could render, he had died in their care. Before he died he told of an ambush: a party of men and women, he could not say how many, were sorely beset. It was in running towards them in a futile gesture that the arrow had taken him. He had collapsed making his way back.

Thomas was even now on the road to Marylesse with as large a party as he could muster, fearing the worst. This was confirmed within the day: none of Davina's party had survived. Pitiful signs were found: one dead beast, a torn pack, arrows in the trees and some articles of female clothing.

Later, they came upon the bodies.

# 4

## August 2008

Scanlon walked with a practised air over the uncertain ground, but with some trepidation. The remains of a stone track, which bore the marks of ironbound wheels on cracked cobbles, took an erratic path into the woodland which had been his companion for the past half mile. It rounded large boulders and outcrops, and was never visible as a continuous stretch for more than a few yards at a time. The soil was a thin crust on the limestone. Into this unyielding landscape the trees sent tough, probing roots splitting the stones, forcing their way to find nourishment for the knotted branches overhead. Between them the leaf-strewn floor did not look stony except for the track itself and where larger boulders broke through the moss. Ground ivy, briars and bracken took a tenuous hold.

The route climbed steadily. Scanlon made his way along it, stepping wide over obstacles, using hands as well as feet where it became steep and rough and the old track disappeared. Twilight was closing in. They had told him in the village that on the higher slopes of the hillside, on which the woodland appeared to hang, was a refuge in which he could pass the night, but it was a long time since he had left the moorland and entered this confusing, tree-strewn wilderness.

The little daylight that filtered through to the stone track thinned as the gloom of the trees closed in. Eventually, and with great reluctance, he stopped, unable to see his footing any more. He would have to pass the night in the open, after all. Searching by touch and using the last of the fading light he found a relatively smooth patch at the foot of one of the twisted trees. He moved one or two stones but found that tugging rocks out of the ground made an even rougher surface. In some discomfort and low spirits he half lay and half leaned against the tree. As the air chilled he tugged his clothes around him and closed his eyes.

There were few noises in the wood. He was more tired than he realised, but sleep in such circumstances is a fitful thing, competing with the cold and the insistent pressure of the stones, and filled with gibberish dream-sounds and meaningless images.

Suddenly he was fully awake, staring into the dark towards a sound that was not part of his dreams. Something was coming up the track. For a moment he saw the glow of a light among the tree stems and heard the clatter of stone against stone.

He stood up – it fell quiet again – and then unmistakably, the sound of footsteps. He called, 'Hello!'

Silence and darkness. He called again, trying to put a reassuring note into his voice. 'Hello! Is anyone there? I'm lost!'

Silence again. Was there a faint glow among the trees? He tried again more loudly, 'I don't want to alarm you but I need your help. I seem to have lost my way.'

'Stay there. I'm coming.'

The voice seemed very far away. He waited, pulling his clothes around him as the chill air penetrated more deeply. Presently the glow grew brighter and again he heard the sound of feet against stone. Suddenly the light of a lamp appeared close at hand, but dazzled by, it he could see no one.

'Are you all right? What are you doing here?'

'I've missed my way. I was looking for the refuge hut to pass the night.'

'Refuge hut? If you mean St Anselm's you're not lost; it's close at hand, but you would have found it shut. I will take you; I have the key.'

'You're very kind.'

He could see the speaker's face now, weather-beaten and lined, with a short beard. As they proceeded up the steepening track, Scanlon introduced himself: 'Frank Scanlon. I'm really pleased you came along.'

His companion made no acknowledgement but raised his lamp. 'Nearly there.'

'I thought I would have to spend the night in the woods. I was trying to get some sleep when I heard you come.'

'Sleep? Time enough for sleep later. Here we are – hold the lamp.'

They stood before a large solid door in a stone wall, which seemed to rise out of the ground like one of the many outcrops that projected into the woods. He held the lantern, which was oil fired, while his companion turned a large key in an apparently unoiled lock and swung back the door. Taking back the lamp he stood it on a high shelf inside the door and motioned to Scanlon to sit on a wooden settle beside the grate while he kindled a fire. A pot on a swivelled arm was filled with water and swung over the fire, and within fifteen minutes they were drinking from steaming mugs, and candles had been lit.

'I suppose there is no electricity out here,' ventured Scanlon.

His companion regarded him steadily for several seconds and looked him up and down. Finally, shaking himself like a man waking, he reached into a pouch at his waist and said, without withdrawing his hand, 'I know you must be tired but I wonder if we might talk for a while. You see, I am also a traveller – of a sort.'

Scanlon thought, not for the first time, how much like a monk he looked. 'Are you a monk?'

'I was. I don't know what I am now. Your clothes – the cloth is very fine…'

His companion embarked on a somewhat quizzical, not to say querulous, assessment of Frank: his clothes, his hair, his backpack (this came in for particular scrutiny). Then he suddenly broke off with an unexpected question. 'What year is it?'

'Don't you know?'

'Let's say I don't.'

'It's 2008.'

'2008… 2008… 2008…' he kept repeating it to himself in a puzzled manner. Then – 'Do you believe in ghosts?'

'No. That is, I don't know. When you woke me on the path I had a few moments of irrational fear.'

'Do you believe in anything? I mean, do any beliefs you have greatly affect your life?' He had the air of struggling to say something other than what he was actually coming out with, and finding the words inadequate. Firelight flared orange on the walls with sudden flashes of gold. Throughout their talk the stranger had been holding something clasped in his hand that he had drawn from the pouch. Now he held it out, extending his fingers so that it lay on his flat palm for inspection. Scanlon saw a small, dull grey pebble, well rounded and worn, like a pebble you would find in a riverbed or on a beach.

'What do you see?'

'A stone.'

'Look closer.'

He reached out to take it but the stranger snapped his fingers shut defensively. Then, as though immediately relenting, he opened them again and placed the stone on the low table before the fire.

'Don't touch it just yet, but examine it more closely.'

Scanlon peered at it in the candle and firelight. It was superficially a small, grey, rounded stone little more than three inches across, but on close inspection it was not actually grey but white with a scattering of black flecks of varying sizes, like thinly scattered dust. The closer he looked, the more flecks he saw so that he could not actually find a clear area of white: this gave it an elusive quality. He felt that if the flecks were cleared away the stone would be very bright indeed, perhaps even painful to look at.

'Is it dusty?' he asked, but the question was rhetorical. Transferring his gaze to the black particles themselves he caught glints and reflections of the firelight. There was a sense of depth to them. Were they pits or bumps on the surface? He shut one eye then the other, trying to fix on them, but even the largest presented such a confusion of reflections and blackness differently to each eye that he could not pin them down. His eyes were distracted between the white of the stone, the blackness of the flecks, and reflections like a sky full of stars.

'It is confusing.' He looked up. His host was watching him intently. 'What is it?'

'I don't know. I was given it when...' he paused and relaunched his sentence: 'I know what it is for. It is a Namestone. Its properties are unique, but I do not know what it is made of or where it is from. It influences me and I find I can influence it.'

'Show me.'

'You are tired and the night is passing on. We will talk in the morning when we are both rested.'

The next day dawned cloudy but bright with a light breeze. Scanlon folded the blankets that the monk had supplied the night before and made his way out of the small room he had been allocated, along a narrow corridor to a spiral stairway that took him down to the room in which they had talked the previous night.

There was no sign of his companion but the fire was still burning. There was a pot of water keeping warm beside it that contained two hard-boiled eggs which, with the bread and butter that was on the table and a jug of cold water, made a passable breakfast.

The door was open. Following a busy knocking sound he rounded the corner of the building to find the monk stacking cut firewood in a small outhouse. With a 'Good morning,' he joined in, and they exchanged the usual morning pleasantries. Once the wood was stacked they returned to the building and sat outside on a low bench, enjoying the morning air.

'I feel at quite a disadvantage not knowing your name,' said Scanlon after a pause.

After a further pause the other answered, 'I do not mean to be rude, but on taking vows, a monk renounces his old name along with his possessions and takes, or is given, another which is used for the rest of his life unless he chooses another... but I no longer choose to use my vow-name, and my birth-name, Simon, belongs to another world and another time.

'I suppose that as this is St. Anselm's you could call me Anselm. Don't worry! I am no saint!'

'Very well, Anselm it is. Anselm, I'm pleased to know you.'

'And welcome to my house, Frank.'

They sat quietly as the clouds began to break up and the sun came and went. Anselm's strange behaviour the previous night had left Scanlon with many questions, and this further revelation increased the unanswered puzzles. 'You said the stone was a Namestone?'

'Yes, or so I was told. It has healing properties if used rightly, or perhaps I should say comforting, strengthening ones. I have great reason to be grateful for that. Without it I would have been utterly unmade.'

'What do you mean?'

Anselm made no answer.

'You said, "*if used rightly*". How do you use it?'

'Not in the utilitarian sense, but to treat it well, to trust it, to guard it.'

'Guard it? From what?'

Again Anselm did not answer but stood and took a few paces forwards in the sunlight. Then he turned and looked up at the house. 'I never thought I'd see this again. Do you fancy a walk?'

'I thought you lived here. Yes, a walk by all means.'

They went uphill, leaving the door unlocked and open. 'The house is safe; nothing can touch it now,' said Anselm in answer to Scanlon's concern.

The darkness of the previous evening was not the least in evidence as they walked through the glowing green and gold shade of trees overhead. Birds called and bright insects hummed by, and somewhere ahead the sough of the wind in the trees competed with the rush of a stream. As they pressed on in silence, the sound of the stream came and went with the twists and turns of the path, louder each turn until on one turn, high up through the trees they caught the distinct glimpse of a waterfall. Before they reached it Anselm turned suddenly off the main track onto an overgrown path to the right. They struggled somewhat with the undergrowth which had taken advantage of the path's evident disuse to send tendrils and briars snaking across it in an attempt to reclaim it for the wood.

They picked their way cautiously for about a hundred yards and came out into a bright level clearing of which the main feature was a broad pool just too small to be called a lake. The sound of falling water filled their ears, but although he could see the outflow, where the pool issued as a tumbling stream between steep rocks, he could not see how it was fed. There was no picturesque cascade tumbling into it, and the waterfall he had glimpsed earlier was nowhere to be seen. Where one might expect to see one the rocks rose sheer but dry in a small cliff.

'It is fed from its depths,' said Anselm. 'The stream above disappears into limestone fissures and somehow supplies the pool. If you swim you can sometimes feel the upwelling water.'

They sat at the waterside on the dry trunk of a fallen tree as the ground was too moist. For a long time neither spoke. They listened to the water and the birds, and enjoyed the sun.

Suddenly, in a somewhat clipped manner, Anselm said, 'I'm going to swim.'

Glancing at him as he rose, Scanlon thought he wiped his eyes. Stripping off, the monk placed his clothes in a pile with the pouch underneath and half slipped, half jumped into the pool. Moments later Scanlon joined him, and they thrashed around in the water, splashing and laughing. The water was cool but not chilly, and as long as they kept moving it was not too cold. Away from the slope where they had sat it was quite deep enough for swimming.

Lacking towels, they brushed off as much water as possible and, after dressing, walked briskly back. Scanlon, noticing that Anselm now carried the pouch in his hand, asked how the risk in leaving it near the pool when swimming squared with his professed duty to guard it. 'Even with no one about there are animals, magpies. Something might have happened to it.'

'It was safe,' said Anselm. 'Safer than it is now. Don't ask me how I knew; somehow it tells me.'

'It tells you things? You mean to say that somehow that stone knows whether it is safe or not, and tells you?'

'Something like that. Actually it is altogether safe in itself. Nothing untoward can happen to it. It is the relationship between it and me that is at risk, but not when I was in the pool.'

'Even a stone can be damaged; nothing is altogether safe.'

'You do not understand!' Anselm's tone was suddenly angry. 'That can be dangerous. We are back now. Have you a change of clothes? These are damp.'

Scanlon went to his room and took a change of clothing from his pack. Returning downstairs to dry his clothing before the fire, he found Anselm already changed and setting his own

25

clothes out. The pouch was once again fastened around his waist.

Scanlon looked at him thoughtfully. 'These clothes need drying. I should have asked, do you mind my staying another day?'

'Of course. I had rather taken it for granted. Last night you were very tired and I kept you awake with foolish questions.'

'Not at all. I was interested. Thank you for showing me the Namestone.'

Anselm's face clouded. 'That may have been a mistake. It is not of casual interest.'

'I'm sorry if I seemed casual – it is a thing of some mystery.'

'Some.' He was unwilling to discuss it further. 'Perhaps you would like to work for your keep. I have wood to cut. The stock is low.'

Scanlon agreed willingly. They took turns outside sawing and chopping a stack of long stems, taking them by the barrow-load to the outhouse log pile to be stacked later. The work was hot and they stripped to the waist as the long timbers were reduced to manageable fire-logs and tipped by the store pile.

After a long, heavy stint of chopping, Scanlon laid down the axe, the timber pile finished. Anselm loaded the last logs onto the barrow and trundled them round the house to the log pile. Presently, instead of his return, Scanlon heard once more the busy sound of logs being stacked. Feeling he had more than earned his keep, he sat back and listened to the steady sound of Anselm at the pile. Beside him were their two piles of clothes and the pouch.

# 5

In his relaxed state the sound of stacking wood was almost hypnotic. Birds sang out of sight in trees, which lifted and lowered their branches with a sighing sound. Time seemed to hang in a harmony of nature blended with a deeper, almost subsonic music. Was it his own breathing? Or the coursing of his blood? He closed his eyes and the sound grew in his ears like the deep notes of an organ, falling, falling... *'It hath a dying fall.'*

He opened his eyes. Somehow the whole of nature seemed to tune itself to the note as though the sound was the true nature. The birds' song, the breeze and Anselm's work seemed no more than bright harmonies on the surface. He was sure it was not his own breathing and pulse – they were there too, but just another part of the dance on the surface of nature. That resonating, organic rise and fall... if there was such a thing as the music of the spheres, this must be the nearest thing to it.

What the devil was it? He had ruled out anything like a distant waterfall – it was too insistently close, too much a part of everything. Why had he not heard it before? It had too deep a note to pin down its direction. Its depth made it all pervading, palpable rather than audible.

It was the pouch: not the pouch itself, but the Namestone within it.

Scanlon could not tell how he knew, only that he did. It was immediately and thoroughly self-evident. Like a puzzle picture that suddenly changes in the seer's eye from a chaotic jumble to a distinct image, he knew the sound was a purposeful note, like a summoning bell. He reached over and felt the pouch, expecting to feel it throb beneath his touch, but there was nothing, only the greater certainty that this was the centre of things.

It was definitely a summons, without losing any of its quality of being the underlying motive of his surroundings. Was it calling Anselm? The sound of his work at the log store continued unabated. Could it only be heard by the person being called? If so...

But that was impossible! The stone was not his; the pouch was not his. Anselm had been reluctant for him to touch it and later even to talk about it. The call became a rushing in his ears. He was suddenly seized by the image that he had had of it the previous night, as a sky full of stars. It swam before him, imbued with the sound so that for the moment the whole universe seemed to be calling him. Dazed, he loosened the pouch string and felt inside. At first nothing, then, feeling a pocket within, he felt for and found the stone and made to draw it out.

How heavy it was! It seemed to resist his pull, not so much like a dead weight, but like a heavy barge in water. Slowly it seemed to gain momentum and come with him. As it did so he had one of the strange losses of perspective that one gets on looking down from a bridge on to a moving river. It was as though he and his surroundings moved and the stone was still. Recovering himself, he drew it towards him and held it on his outstretched palm as Anselm had done the night before.

He peered at it again, the interplay of white stone and reflective grains. This time, as there was no firelight, the reflections must be those of the sky and the landscape. He studied one of the larger flecks and found that, like the white areas of stone, it was confusingly interlaced with whiteness as the white had been with flecks. He was conscious of looking at one dark area but could not say where it ended and where white stone began. He looked at the reflections in it.

Once, as a child stepping over a broad puddle, he had glimpsed the reflections of the trees above his head and felt a sudden sense of vertigo as they seemed to sway way beneath him. The same thing happened now. He lost all sense of the smallness of the stone. His eyes were very close to it but the reflections (were they reflections?) remained clear. The shadow of his head did not affect them in the least. They moved and swirled and streamed past him in a nonsense pattern, but not altogether nonsense – he had fleeting glimpses of the trees and the house, and then he lost them in the general swirl of light and dark. Then a fence – gone again! – and Anselm working at the outhouse. He leaped back in shock, looking towards the sound of the logs. But the outhouse was around the corner of the building, out of sight. He could not see Anselm, nor could Anselm see him – how then could he be reflected?

Cautiously he peered again at the stone but was unable to find the large fleck he had looked at before. Where was it? Unsuccessful, he settled for the largest he could find but it was smaller and harder to see into. Nevertheless, the closer he peered, the larger it seemed to grow. Once more there was a confusion of light and images. Fleetingly he glimpsed the log store but from a different angle, and lost it again just as quickly. Images of trees came and went, and suddenly the path on which he and Anselm had approached the house, and which he knew to be on the far side. He looked to discover whereabouts on the path it was, and the image remained. He could see where it disappeared down the hill into the trees and rocks. Instinctively he leaned to see around the bend. His viewpoint changed and for a moment he felt he could see the next bend as it swept by in the swirl of images caused by his movement. He froze, and the images fell apart into a meaningless jumble.

Eventually he found that he could only see properly when he was relaxed and still, and that either sudden movement or tense freezing ruined his view. Once he held a picture, however, he could shift his viewpoint by a calm movement, little more than that produced by breathing. In fact, the first few times he did this he simply breathed himself into a slightly adjusted viewpoint.

Again he found the footpath, and in this relaxed mode he easily moved along it. Sometimes he found he could travel in an apparently normal way, progressing from one point to another, and at other times he somehow faded from one place to the next. He noticed that this was where he recognised a place on the path that he had seen the previous night by the light of Anselm's lamp. At such times the normal 'pressure' of motion carried him immediately to the new place. He could turn and look back, and once retraced his route for a short distance and turned again. This time, by deliberately thinking about the intervening path he could travel on it normally, but as soon as he concentrated on the known place ahead he arrived there.

He wondered if he might find the place where he had slept, but was distracted by a bright flickering of light above him. Looking up he saw it was a squirrel disturbing the leaves, but as he looked his viewpoint again moved – this time upwards to the patch of sky between the leaves. Momentarily startled, he intensified his gaze, only to find that his viewpoint began to rush out of control in a flood of light. Slowly he turned his gaze and found himself viewing from far above the wood – he could see the moorland track below. He had no sense of flying, even as he realised he had had no sense of travelling through the wood – only that of viewing and moving his point of view. The squirrel that had disturbed the leaves made no sound that he had heard. The sounds he received were still those of his known surroundings – Anselm at the log pile and the birds around the house.

Looking down at the moorland path he saw, far away, a movement on it and, again setting his viewpoint in motion, came towards it. It was a group of three men coming steadily up the path. One, obviously in charge, was wearing a rust-coloured, almost mediaeval jerkin and a gown like Anselm's, open at the front. Suddenly he looked up, as though he was looking directly into Scanlon's eyes, and drew back his lips in an evil, aggressive leer.

Startled, Scanlon lost control. In a rush of light and shadow he found himself back at St Anselm's with the stone no longer on his palm but clenched tightly in his fist. He pushed it back roughly into the pouch and, feeling again that strange sense of resistance to its movement, hastily closed it.

What had he seen? What had happened? Until the last moment it had seemed as though he had been observing events remotely as though on, or more correctly in, a television screen – not that there had been any suspicion or indication of gadgetry about it. The stone had a mysterious, self-sufficient quality of its own. Throughout he had not felt part of the scene in the stone: he had been an observer only, until that last moment. Could the man on the path really have seen him? He had looked straight into his eyes, or was that a chance accident? If so, who else could that look have been intended for? He had been viewing from above: had the man raised his offensive sneer to the heavens? Something in the thought made his blood chill.

The problem was, what to do now? The only person who could possibly give answers was Anselm, but he could hardly tell him he had been rifling his pouch – could he? Following the sound of stacking logs he walked around the building to see – with some embarrassment – that the work was all but finished.

'I'm sorry, I should have helped.'

'Not at all. You did your stint with the axe.'

Scanlon passed Anselm the last few logs. Afterwards they strolled round to the front of the house and sat on the bench. 'Anselm, I need to talk to you.'

'Go ahead, there's little else to do.'

'About the stone…'

'Yes, forgive my brusqueness earlier. You must understand it is a very personal subject, and one of which I have only a partial understanding. I'm not sure how to begin.'

'The stone calls.'

Anselm looked at him sharply. 'You heard it?'

'Yes.'

'Did you respond?'

'I'm afraid so. Yes.'

There was a long pause during which Scanlon realised he was holding his breath. Anselm broke it: 'Yes, you would have to.' A longer pause, then: 'The stone has authority. I don't know how but I feel it can compel, although it has never done so before, or not in its present form. You would have to be very determined or very obtuse not to respond to it. My surprise is that it would call you, or that you could hear it. Perhaps I shouldn't be. You are probably the reason for its – my – being here.'

'It was lucky for me that you came along when you did.'

'It was not luck I was sent.'

'But you live here.'

Anselm looked around and took a deep comfortable breath, but which ended with a frown. 'Once I did, but no longer.'

'You have the key.'

'I always have the key, but I have another home now. Perhaps I always had and this was just a lodging.'

'In the monastery.'

'What monastery?' Anselm stood up with a sign of his earlier ill temper. 'There is no monastery.'

'I'm sorry, I thought you said —'

'How did you respond to the Namestone?'

'I took it out of your pouch and looked at – into – it.'

'That was very dangerous.'

'I think I had no choice. I saw you working – and the path down from St Anselm's.' He went on to describe how he had learned to control the stone, although Anselm scowled his disagreement at that way of putting it. But when he came to the three men, and particularly the man in the russet jerkin, he was pressed hard for a detailed description.

'Tall and thickset; short, grizzled, dark hair; a slightly hunched appearance as he walked. He took long steps and the other two kept up as well as they could.' Describing the man's aggressive leer, he said, 'I couldn't tell if it was directed to me or to heaven.'

'Hérault.' said Anselm. 'I knew him. If he had known you were there – which he could not because strictly you were not – then it might have been for you, but no, it was certainly for heaven.'

'You know him? Well, he is on his way here.'

'No. He died when the monastery was destroyed. The Namestone shows the totality of things past and things present. He did come up that path long ago, but never again.'

'But I saw him just now on the moor.'

'The Namestone shows the entirety of all things, now and in the past, and perhaps sometimes the future as well. You are not sufficiently skilled in its use to choose or control what you see. It is very difficult for me: I feel I owe you some explanation and yet I understand so little myself. Yesterday I asked you if anything you believed affected your way of life. Perhaps I should have put it differently, but belief and being, where does one begin?'

'I am afraid I only have beliefs of a practical nature – some things are of use or pleasant in everyday life; others are better avoided. The supernatural leaves me cold.'

'I am, or was, the same – now I don't know where I stand. The Namestone changed everything.'

'I don't know what that device is or how it works, but one thing I am sure of: a competent scientist could analyse it and tell me.'

'Perhaps one could.' Anselm paused.

After a while Scanlon said, 'You are sure that thing records the past as well as the present? Your Mr Hérault looked pretty present to me.'

'Totally sure. I was... present... at his death.'

Anselm stood up from the bench, then sat down again. Presently he began to recount the story of himself and Hérault.

# 6

'After the dissolution of the monasteries by Henry VIII, the monks and acolytes suffered many and varied fates. Some returned to their founding monasteries overseas; some, unwisely resisting the secular authority, met unpleasant ends. Goods and lands became forfeit to the crown. Many who had lived lives of greater or lesser length found themselves thrown into secular life. Those few monastic groups that remained no longer enjoyed ecclesiastical authority and protection and were without land and property. If they survived it was because they were too small and too poor to attract attention or be perceived as a threat to the king. They were reclusive gatherings rather than monasteries.

'Of those who went out into the world at large there were understandably many who had never entirely shared the religious convictions of their fellows but who had opted for a protected and secure livelihood in uncertain times. Some of these found the outside world an unsettling place – often too much so for one who had totally adapted to the cloistered life. They were like souls in limbo with no home in either place.

'Some of the small groups that remained accepted these wanderers back into the fold, but it was not easy. The nature of the break-up of their previous way of life brought many things out into the open. Monks who had lost faith rubbed shoulders with those who professed it and with still others whose faith had been not only held but strengthened. Some of these groups, though small, became a hotchpotch of debate on the necessity and nature of faith.

'All this is now centuries ago, but it opened the door to a far more open and aware religious life. But in by the same door came self-seeking and unscrupulous men, drawn by tales of riches that had escaped Henry's clutches. If a monastic group had survived, why had it? If it was growing, why was it? To some men there was only a venial answer. They were fuelled by tales, some true and some false, of churches grown fat on tithes, which after the dissolution had become societies hoarding untold wealth: secret caches, buried gold and chalices, crucifixes and relics with supernatural powers which could in their turn confer wealth and power on those who possessed them. In one form or another these tales, often disguised as fiction, have survived. There are many so-called guardians of the Holy Grail, or whatever gloss legend puts upon it.

'Such a rumour drew Hérault to the small monastery of St Antipas-in-Pergamon to which this old lodge of St Anselm's belonged. I too was drawn here, though for different reasons. It is enough to say that fate had taken a hand in my life in equal proportion to that by which God had withheld his, and I had resolved to force God's hand or perish in defying it. Hérault's motives and mine were very similar. We had both said, "There is no God, or if there is…" only in Hérault's case the sentence finished, "… if there is I shall use him." And in mine it was, "… if there is I shall hate him." Perhaps the intentions were more similar than the words implied.

'I have said the community in St Antipas-in-Pergamon was small. We were just fifteen souls – too few for any division of labour or for any structured hierarchy. Of the fifteen, about half a dozen were temporary lodgers, including Hérault and myself. Our numbers thus fluctuated by two or three as men came and went. "Temporary", you must understand, is relative to the lifelong commitment of the core of monks. At the time I am talking about, Hérault and I had both been there for more than six months; I rather longer than he. Others stayed for a month or more and some were literally weekenders, bringing our total occasionally to twenty, but as I said, at the time we were fifteen.

'Apart from the daily offices and observances and the routine of running the establishment, there were sessions of debate, of private study and of joint study – that is to say, study and debate in pairs or within small groups or with one of the permanent monks. I hasten to say that this was a licence taken rather than promoted, as it was a marked departure from the strict and, as it proved, necessary discipline of the order. The influence of the order itself was, since Henry, noticeable only by its absence.

'Presumably because we had some common ground which we could not altogether share with the brethren, Hérault and I became regular partners in our wider studies. In all of these private discussions, as I later came to see, Hérault gave little away but learned much about me and my private doubts and hates. He somehow seemed to convey the air of holding orthodox views while at the same time sympathising and encouraging revolt in me. Only occasionally, and recognised only in retrospect, did his mask slip.

'Occasionally our talk turned to mundane things like maintenance and the day-to-day running of the order. Then he would set little puzzles before me that, purely from lack of inside knowledge, I could not answer. What reserves does the order have against the unforeseen? Are we just a group preserving eternal truths? Or is something else guarded here against the day of the restoration of the monasteries? Does the order look for restoration? Surely in an unbelieving age something must be done to restore what is being lost daily? What power holds it all together? Money? Something less tangible? He hinted at powers and dominations of a supernatural order but in such a way that I could only infer his devoutest meaning while somehow providing a frisson of darker undertones myself. God? The Holy Spirit? Why, yes of course, but the mechanics of spirituality in the world must surely use worldly means to have any tangible effect. Is the

Holy Spirit the only spirit to be considered? After all, God is a spirit and those who worship him must worship in spirit. If we can do that, we must be spirits ourselves by nature, and if us, then what others? What of angels? What of demons?

'Looking back, I see the seductive undercurrent, but at the time all was companionable and open. The dark side seemed to be all mine own, kept secret and apart. I thought myself slightly superior, as though I could see what he could not, the awful truth behind the gilded appearance. Now I see that I was led, but not guiltless: I let myself be led.

'The Prior appointed Phillip, one of the permanent monks, as my spiritual director. I went to him after Matins if it was not my time for other duties, and such had been my understanding and quick response to teaching that I was moving steadily towards acceptance of full brotherhood in the order. Now with the guileful prompting of Hérault I combined my progress towards initiation with all the cunning inquiry that he with greater cunning practised on me. He had come convinced that this particular community concealed either great treasure or the secret of great power, or both. I performed his work for him in rooting it out.

'Where he had wormed his information from, I knew not. By what means, or what degrees, he came to this monastery, I have no idea, but perhaps I was, in my hatred of God, ready to be convinced of all manner of deceit in his servants.

'There was truth in Hérault's conviction, and I uncovered it.

'They say love and hate are close allies. That may be, but I know that in spite of the evil motives that fuelled me I progressed through the paths of both initiation and devious discovery, concealing my true feelings and convincing the brotherhood of my spiritual suitability and genuine faith. The nearest description of my state is that of the devils who also believe and tremble, except that I did not – God help me – tremble. Or if I did, it was with anger against the hand of God as I had seen it in my life to date. The brothers discerned it as fervour.'

Anselm stood and looked up at the clouds sailing above us to the north. In the quiet that followed I heard the sharp cries of birds in the woods, far away. Chi-chi-chi-chi-chi! Then it was birdsong again and wind in the trees. After a long pause, Anselm continued.

'By the end of a twelve-month in the monastery I became a fully fledged monk with a new name, and I was possessed of the knowledge that was to destroy both it and Hérault, as well as – save for an act of grace – myself.

'The state of the community of St Antipas-in-Pergamon was pitifully reduced from that of its parent in the middle ages when it had numbered its adherents in hundreds if not thousands. Its sphere of influence was contracted from the whole western seaboard of Europe to this tiny mountainside. Its links with Rome were severed. Its spirit should have died long ago. But it survived.

'Had it been no more than the flickering flame that it seemed to be, it should have guttered and died. There should have been nothing to maintain the interest of an intellect like Hérault's for a day, let alone a year. There should have been nothing for me to find. But Antipas-in-Pergamon was a guardian of more than it seemed. Nine days after my initiation as the ninth brother in the community I was taken to a small chamber in the Sanctuary of the chapel.

'I should have mentioned the chapel before. Like the rest of the buildings, it was in serious disrepair. Certain parts were in a physically dangerous state. Windows and doorways had been filled in, remade, repositioned. Stones had crumbled and mortar was often non-existent. The altar was barely recognisable; its patched and threadbare hangings would not have graced a scullery. The initiates – the monks – who guarded it, with the exception of two, and now with me, three, were old and, although wise and filled with sanctity and reverence, they were also too filled with years to do more than maintain the daily observances and teaching. The two younger brothers were consequently responsible for the day-to-day running of the house and the care of noviciates and boarders. No time was left for rebuilding and repairs.

'With me, they intimated, perhaps there was a chance to remedy this, and later with Hérault, well – who knows?

'Who indeed?

'Then they brought me to the Sanctuary – not that in the chapel, but another.

'I had not even known of its existence as it was not accessed directly from within the chapel but from one of the rooms nearby. There was no door, but a stone, hidden behind a pile of smaller stones like builder's debris, rolled in a channel to reveal an opening that led to a room glowing with orange lamplight. As soon as I entered I was aware that the ruinous nature of the rest of the building did not extend to here. The stones were not only sound but they gleamed in the light as though freshly cut from the quarry and newly set in place. The lamps and their wall fittings shone with polished copper and brass, their glasses bright, clear and unsooted. The vaulted roof was of perfect proportions and almost appeared to be suspended over the fresh-smelling air like trees in a forest suddenly stilled, likely to move in the slightest breeze yet strong and able to stand for centuries.

'The air was fresh but filled with a heavy, heady fragrance that did not come from the lamps. Six of the monks had gone ahead of me into the Sanctuary and I followed with Phillip and one of the younger monks, so that at first I could not see the centre of the Sanctuary. It easily accommodated us and would have held at least a dozen more. Finally we formed a circle around a central altar, a square table on which a small earthenware jar stood with a white cloth set around it in a horseshoe shape. The jar had a long tapering neck which was broken near the top; the broken top lay before it between the open arms of the cloth horseshoe. These arms draped or spilled over the edge of the altar and hung for a few inches as though pouring down at my feet. There were hairs clinging to the neck of the jar.

'What followed was at the same time sacramental and mundane. A small service was held with these relics and myself as a sort of double focus. The service itself was unremarkable, almost boring. Reverence was made, under God, to the relics, which were not named, and I promised to guard and protect them against some future time. Well-known versicles and responses were said; we knelt or stood according to known patterns and towards the end I was invited to kneel while the hands of the brothers were laid upon my head and shoulders. After a few concluding sentences we left as we had come, and the stone was rolled back as though sealing a tomb. Phillip remained behind.

'That was the mundane outward event that somehow the worldly part of me observed as an outsider, curious and calculating. The Sanctuary was in good order, well preserved but simple. Its fittings and embellishments showed an excellent degree of craftsmanship and quality but were of a plain rather than a rich nature. There were no bejewelled or gilded trappings, nothing a venial man might desire. The jar was exquisitely made, but at the same time utilitarian, and it was broken. The cloth was a cloth. Someone, part of me observed, should have cleaned the hairs from the broken neck of the jar.'

Anselm shifted on the bench and was about to say more when the summer air was broken by an oath and clattering of stones. Hérault, whom I had seen in the stone, and whom Anselm had proclaimed dead, strode brusquely out of the woods.

41

# 7

The effect on Anselm was dramatic and horrific. His face turned the grey-green pallor of death. He made as if to rise but slid forwards off the bench onto his knees. Hérault strode brusquely to stand over him and spat in his face. Anselm seemed not to notice: his gaze was that of a man seeing other things; things seen in his mind only, almost too much for him to bear.

The ludicrous parody of Paul on the Damascus road kneeling before Christ thrust itself into Scanlon's mind. Sunshine glittered in the spittle on Anselm's face and for a moment there was absolute silence – not a bird, not a breath of air.

Then a cloud hid the sun, and with a violent and angry cry Anselm burst to his feet, grasping Hérault under his arms with such force that he lifted him from his feet. The two rose bodily together, Anselm to his full six feet with Hérault a foot above him. The imbalance was too great and they crashed heavily to the ground. Hérault's knee came up into the pit of Anselm's stomach. Scanlon leaped forwards, uncertain what he should be doing, but he never arrived. Just as he saw Hérault bring his clasped hands down on the back of Anselm's head, his own vision burst into stars, darkness and pain.

\* \* \*

His face was wet and cold; he could not open his eyes – the pain in the back of his skull seared through his brain to his eyes, clamping them shut. Water dripped from his hair onto his forehead and brows. Sudden and cold, a drench of water crashed onto his chest. Someone was keeping him upright, holding his arms. He lifted his head, eyes still shut.

'Ha! He's coming round! Hold him up!'

Slowly he opened his eyes a crack, but they were too wet to be able to see. He received another shock of water in his face. He tried to speak but water poured into his throat, making him cough and retch. He was thrust down onto his knees and sat back on his heels. Someone grabbed his hair. The pain in his head was unbearable.

'Now, my pretty! There, there, my pretty! Time to wake up now.'

The hand in his hair rocked him slowly from side to side and his eyes slowly opened to reveal Hérault's face inches from his own.

'There, now, are we awake?'

'Who are you?'

'What? Didn't your friend tell you? Stephen and I have shared so much together, surely he told you about me?'

'You are Hérault. Where is Anselm?'

'Sit him on the bench!'

Hands seized his arms and dragged him backwards, pushing him roughly onto the bench that he and Anselm had been sitting on earlier. Scanlon saw a man on each side of him; one, sharp faced and vicious looking; the other thickset and dull. They held him fast. Hérault took a couple of paces forwards but remained about six feet away.

'I am rather hoping you will be able to help me. You see, I have come a very long way for a very special purpose and I am sure you will want to avoid any further misunderstandings by being as helpful as you can.'

'Where is Anselm?'

'Anselm? Hah! Another name change? Simon, Stephen, Anselm – well, it doesn't matter. I am afraid he fared rather worse than you. Fenster and Harpin here are just too good at their job.'

'I told him you were coming – he didn't believe me.'

'A pity for him. So you knew I was coming.'

'I saw you but he said you were dead.'

For a moment Hérault's manner faltered and his face paled in an echo of Anselm's when he strode out of the wood. Then he drew back his lips in the sneer Scanlon had seen before.

'Death! What is death? Look around you – all nature dies but the world goes on. Some of us have no time for death; there are more important things.' He regarded Scanlon quizzically for a few seconds. 'And who are you, my friend?'

'My name's Frank Scanlon. I asked you, where is Anselm?'

'All in good time. When and where did you see me?'

'From a long way off, on the moor.' Scanlon determined not to mention the stone. Who would believe it anyway?

'And yet you were all cosy chatting to our monkish friend after we had struggled up through this blasted forest. A good runner, eh?'

Scanlon said nothing.

'So this is all that remains of Antipas-in-Pergamon?'

Hérault walked round him and stood facing the building. 'Let him go!' he turned, and then to Scanlon: 'Come here.'

Scanlon got up and walked unsteadily forward until they both stood before the door of the old building. Hérault paused a moment, musing.

'St Anselm's was the visitor's lodge to the old monastery. So he took its name? As good a name as any. The monastery would not reveal its secrets so… perhaps it is here. Perhaps that is why he used its name.'

'I have never seen the monastery, and don't know anything about this old house. I was just staying the night. Where is Anselm?'

'Where indeed? A nice philosophical question which I don't propose to answer. The question is, are you going to help me where "Anselm" failed? Perhaps you need time to consider.'

'Time? To help you? You've beaten me up – you and your thugs – and God knows what you've done to Anselm.'

'God knows? There you go with your philosophy again. But I have other business.' He turned to his accomplices. 'Stick him in here: he can be finding all his answers while we search the buildings. When you come out you can decide whether to help us, if your help is still needed, or whether to follow your philosophy.'

He opened the door and produced Anselm's key. Harpin thrust Scanlon inside and he heard the key turn in the lock. Inside, in the thin light that filtered through the shutters, he saw complete devastation. How long had he been unconscious? The room had been stripped, every item turned over, smashed; floorboards had been ripped up; even the contents of the hearth were scattered over the floor. Upstairs was the same: his clothes and backpack had been ripped and scattered and the room wrecked. He went into Anselm's room where he again met the same devastation. Even the bed was turned over, leaning on something underneath it. He took hold of the upturned legs and heaved it over. Underneath, the body of Anselm lay congealed in blood.

# 8

Scanlon staggered out of the room and was sick on the stairs. The effort made the pain in his head throb with hammer blows and he nearly passed out. In the lower room he groped for the door but did not have the strength to beat on it. He leant there and gripped the handle. Why beat on it anyway? They had brutally killed Anselm; why draw their attention? He needed time. Still dazed, he turned back to the lower room and began a futile attempt to tidy things until he realised what he was doing, then his actions became a search. The stone? Everything was somehow connected to the stone. Hérault had not mentioned it so perhaps he had not found it, or if he had, had thought it no more than a pebble. But the pouch and stone were nowhere to be seen.

After several minutes he was forced to admit his reluctance to search the most likely place, and with great unease he made his way up to Anselm's room. The body lay where he had left it, the clothes mostly ripped away. There was no pouch. Swallowing and gritting his teeth, Scanlon made a systematic search of the room, to no avail. Then looking back towards the body he spotted a fragment of cloth under the bed. On lifting the bed off the body he had uncovered some fragments on the floor. Reaching underneath he pulled out a broad bloodstained blanket and the cord of the pouch. Frantically scrabbling under the bed he found the pouch itself, barely recognisable, torn along its seam. The stone was not there. His head throbbed and pounded and he half collapsed on the floor, leaning against the bed. His ears were singing a high-pitched whine, and underneath it, rising and falling with the throbbing of his head, resounded a deeper note which seemed to penetrate his whole body, like the fall of deep notes in Widor's 'Toccata'.

*'It hath a dying fall…'*

He looked at Anselm's body. The sound was not in his head; it came from Anselm. It was the same sound with which the stone had called to him from the pouch. Now it was calling again. It must be on or under the body. Dragging the bed aside to give more room, he turned the already stiffening body of Anselm.

Nothing.

The light in the room was beginning to fade. He searched the floor, Anselm's hands, his clothing, every part. Nothing there, and yet the insistent powerful call of the Namestone went on and on. Could Anselm have swallowed it? If so, that was the end – nothing would induce him to search inside the corpse. He searched again - the hands, the clothes, the body and the floor beneath, and all the time the insistent deep harmonic call penetrated to his depths. Finally he collapsed onto the floor in total dejection, half-lying, half leaning against the wall. He was cold and the ache in his head was becoming unbearable. His eyes closed but his vision swirled with meaningless images. He shifted the debris from the floor underneath him. Shapes flitted before his eyes like the flecks in the stone, and lumps on the floor dug into him like stones. The wall was rough and hard.

Suddenly he was fully awake, staring into the dark. For a moment he fancied he was back in the wood the day before, hearing Anselm coming up the path. Momentarily, just as before, he saw a faint glow, but as he moved it vanished. Unidentifiable flickerings in his retina conflicted with the darkness, making it impossible to distinguish the real from the imagined. The debris on the floor confused with the memory of the stones in the woodland floor, the wall with the tree. Only the pain in his head forced the reminder of what had happened outside the monastery building, along with the persistent deep call of the Namestone.

Once more he saw the light, brighter now, but the turning of his head and the movement of his eyes to see it brought on stabbing pains and flashes in his retinas so that he was lost. He could make out nothing. He fought for a sense of direction. He slid across the floor to where he felt the light had been, pointing his head and staring fixedly ahead so he did not have to turn his eyes. Slowly, like picking out the Milky Way on a hazy night, he made out a broad area of light filled with swirling shapes. It seemed on a level with his own eyes and Scanlon reached into its centre. His fingers clasped around the familiar shape of the Namestone. Where had it come from? How could he have missed it?

As his hand closed around it he was aware that his palm and fingers were illuminated by a dancing glow. He grasped it entirely without touching anything else – surely it must be resting on something. Why could he feel nothing around it? He drew it towards him and again felt the strange sensation of being drawn to it as though it was anchored, or more truly, as before, as though it was the true definition of place and all else, himself included, was relative to it.

The calling sound faded and with it the pain in his head and eyes. The pain was still there but now seemed to be of academic interest only. He wondered why Hérault had not returned when it got dark. With the Namestone in his hand he felt safer and able to think. Anselm had said that the stone had strengthening powers, allying strength with comfort. But it had failed him. Somehow the thought did not worry him as much as it should. The stone seemed to reassure by its mere presence. There was something almost human in whatever emanated from it, and whatever it was felt so positive that, even with Anselm lying dead a few feet away, Scanlon felt encouraged.

But Anselm was still dead. Something in his mind fought against the Namestone's reassurance with an almost petulant refusal to be reassured. Anselm was dead, bloodily murdered!

Was this pebble a drug, some sort of panacea, like tablets doctors give to blunt and deaden all sense of grief and bereavement?

It was dark and whatever merciful delay had kept Hérault away this long could not hold him up much longer. He had already tried various windows for an alternative way out but that had just confirmed what he already knew. St Anselm's was designed to be shut up and left for long periods and the windows were shuttered and barred, each pair of shutters with its own lock. Anselm had not opened them and he may not have been able to. There was no cellar and no attic. The upper rooms rose sheer into an upper loft formed by the roof timbers. He determined to search again and made to thrust the Namestone into his pocket. Once again he met that curious resistance, stronger than before. He tried to counter it by moving his breast pocket towards the stone so it needed just a small further movement to slip it in, but at the critical moment an intense brilliance shone through his closed fingers so that the flesh glowed and the summoning note sounded again, almost deafeningly. He cried out with the pain of intense light and sound. 'Alright, damn you! What the hell do you expect me to do?'

'Look! What do you see?' It was Anselm's voice.

He looked in what he fancied was the direction of Anselm's body but it was dark. Whatever the cause of the stone's brilliance, it did not light up the room.

He could not speak.

'Look!' Anselm again.

The sound of his voice was not in the room; it was as though it was in the stone. What was this? Some sort of black magic? Scanlon looked into it. Like the first time it was a bright, almost painful white, with swirling dark flecks, and flecks of white in the dark shapes. He concentrated on the largest of the dark shapes just as he had while Anselm had been stacking logs. It seemed to grow beyond the outer limits of his vision as he looked into it, as though he had immersed himself in it. As it did so he experienced a strange sensation of a mixture of relief and triumph, which seemed to come, like Anselm's voice, from the Namestone itself. Its glow faded; everything was dark.

At first he saw nothing but darkness, then shapes, patches of gloom in the dark. A tree – stones – no, a stone wall, grass in tufts at its base by a gravel path. Like a walker stumbling in the last dim moments of twilight, he tried to move as he had before but with only partial success. Perhaps it was because the light was so poor. He tried looking up but the sky was too overcast. He turned and found himself close up against a wall. Involuntarily he threw up his hand to protect his face and to his absolute shock he grazed his knuckles on the stones. How could he feel them? Of course – he was still in Anselm's room and had reached out against the wall of the room. He drew back and looked around. Was he in the room? The air was different, and the sound, impossibly, was as though he was really out of doors. He was standing on something loose and rough, like gravel; his knuckles were stinging where he had struck the wall. Hadn't he been kneeling when he looked into the stone? Where was it? His hands were empty. Where on earth was he?

Cautiously reaching forward once he again felt the rough stone wall. A nightjar began a long trill somewhere to his right and he shivered in a cold breeze. This was foolish! He turned slowly and took a few careful steps when a sudden parting of the clouds showed a faint sky-glow outlining the roof of the building. Only moments before he had been inside it.

His mind was beginning to spin and he took a deep breath of fresh night air to calm himself. He screwed his eyes tight shut. This was like some irrational dream; when he opened them he would be back in the room.

He took another deep breath and opened his eyes but the freshness of the air and the sounds were definitely those of outdoors, and the night sky was still dimly showing overhead.

Another noise sounded but he could not tell its direction and, afraid of being caught by the return of Hérault and his henchmen, he shrank back against the wall and edged his way sideways. If he was right, from the glimpse he had caught of the main building, he was standing with his back to one of the outhouses on the uphill side. The main building lay between him and the footpath down to safety. He moved carefully forward but froze at the sound of a footfall on gravel. Someone was between him and St Anselm's! Hérault must have placed one of his men on guard and his way was blocked. He backed quietly to the wall and edged to his left. The cold air was clearing his head but his knuckles stung and his hand felt wet. If he remembered aright, the uphill path he had taken to the pool with Anselm lay to his left around the barn. In his present position he was at the mercy of a sudden clearing of the sky and perhaps the moon exposing him to the guard's view. Resisting the impulse to run, he worked his way to the end of the barn with small half paces. There was the noise of footsteps again and, looking towards the house, he was horrified by a sudden brightening of the light.

He could see clearly enough to make out a figure by the door stretching his arms and stamping his feet with apparent boredom. Just as he realised there was enough light to see and be seen, the clouds parted to reveal a brilliant moon and the thickset figure of Harpin. With a sudden decisive movement the man turned and strode towards him. Stepping back, Scanlon found himself at the corner of the wall and turned to run, but found himself blocked by a short length of fencing which stretched all the way to the uphill path. The distance was too great and Harpin would get there first. He wasted precious seconds searching for a foothold to climb over, failed, and turned to fight.

There was an inexplicable silence. Harpin was standing still, making small shrugging movements. A few moments later he heard the sound of him urinating against the wall; after an eternity he saw the man walk back to the doorway. Scanlon turned to make for the path, but as he did so he heard the sound of voices and Hérault and Fenster emerged. Hérault looked to the building and called, 'All quiet?'

Harpin yawned, 'Yeah, not a peep.'

As Hérault and Fenster joined Harpin at the doorway, Scanlon slipped onto the path and, with all caution gone, fled uphill.

He missed the turning to the pool – not that he would have taken it – and shortly after he missed the path. Although the moon remained in a now clearing sky, it was of no use in a shadowy woodland track and he had probably strayed from it long before he realised. Lower down there had been no problem – the undergrowth was so thick that the path was the only way to go, but as he had climbed, the vegetation had become sparser, though still dense overhead, and somewhere he had mistaken one clear spot for the correct way.

Inevitably he slowed down, keeping uphill where possible. The steady routine of walking while warily searching ahead for obstacles and pitfalls so occupied him that he lost his sense of time. The trees gradually thinned and the moon penetrated to give a clearer view of his way, but he was minded of the advice once given to him by a shepherd: 'Moonlight throws tricks and shadows. If I had to search for sheep at night I'd prefer starlight to the moon anytime.' He realised the truth of it that night, unable as he was to distinguish a dip from a ravine until it was almost too late. Frantically he thrust out for a handhold and caught on a thin stem, far too weak to hold him but enough to swing him in an arc which brought him down against the rock face. Scrabbling with his fingers and pressing his body against the slope, he slowed and stopped his descent, gasping a curse. He inched upwards again until he found a footing, and gradually brought himself to a surface where he could stand. From then on he slowed his progress, testing each step carefully.

Moonlight filtered through clouds and trees, throwing long dazzling swathes across every clearing and dark shadows over and around every obstacle. Shadows danced in his peripheral vision and disappeared when he looked directly at them. Clouds took away his sight just as he strained to make sense of the way ahead. The confusion of the day mingled with that of this bewildering moonscape.

Somehow he needed a detached view to try and understand the events of the past day. In the space of a few hours everything substantial seemed to have been swept from under him. He was in grave danger of mistaking moon shadows for monsters, and moonshine for – well – moonshine. What of Anselm's voice in the room? Or was it in the Namestone? Where was the Namestone? He had been concussed beforehand, probably for some hours, and in his highly emotional state after finding Anselm's body anything was possible. But what of his exit from the room? Perhaps he had had a partial blackout and found a way out in a semiconscious state. Perhaps – but his head ached to think, and it was all a scrambled haze anyway.

He resolved to refuse to think or fear anything supernatural concerning the events of the day. As he had said to Anselm, he was sure a competent scientist could analyse the stone and its properties and provide at least a plausible explanation. There had been no denial. Somehow the answers had to be linked to the stone which had been at the centre of every strange event of the last two days. It had to be the key to all this.

He thought of his friend Tim Austin. A lifelong fascination with how the world works and a first-class analytical mind had led Tim to a Master's degree in particle physics. Later, by a route he did not discuss, he had become a controller in the Middle East Department of Intelligence. Possibly neither the bricks and mortar of physics nor the interplay of relationships, ideals and self-interest in Military Intelligence, which, he joked, put the moron in oxymoron, were satisfying in themselves. To everyone's surprise – his own included – he set himself to seeking the mind behind the matter, eventually becoming a lecturer in theological studies at Capel College on the outskirts of Oxford.

Intensely practical and single-minded, this was just the sort of puzzle Tim would relish. But he was several miles away in his Gloucester flat, and might as well be back in Oxford.

He felt a painful crack on his knee and his already bleeding hands. He had come up against a dry stone wall with what appeared to be an animal trough set into it. He tried to dip his hands into the water but met a hard stone lid. Wearily he peered at its shadowed surface but could make nothing out. He was desperately tired but afraid to rest. Without intending to he stood without moving for a full minute. Coming to, he thought out his position. He was lost, but this could be as much an advantage as a peril. The chance of his pursuers finding him was correspondingly diminished. Perhaps he could stop for a short while. Between the trough and the wall was an angle of turf which he could comfortably lean against.

He decided to rest for just a few minutes.

He closed his eyes.

# 9

When he opened his eyes again it was daylight; a chill mist was blowing on his face. His clothes were damp. What had been a clear sky was obscured by clouds through which now and again a hazy blue could still be seen; wracks of cloud moved up the hillside below, streamed over rock outcrops and through the tops of trees. The stone wall and the trough gleamed with damp and myriads of diamond dewdrops clung to the grass lit by a watery sun. It was hard to move his limbs. He struggled awkwardly to his feet and turned to go on. Hérault must have realised he was missing hours ago. Presumably he owed his freedom to having left the path, or possibly they thought he had made his escape downhill.

Uncertain of his route, Scanlon looked about him. He was surrounded by a tangle of stone walls and scrub. Rounding a wall to his right he was brought to a halt by a rocky scar with a drop of a couple of hundred feet, above which the wall rose sheer, presenting a rounded outer face with an inaccessible, defensive appearance.

Moving to his left he was turned back more than once by obstacles he could neither cross nor climb. He had to skirt the entire labyrinth and was slowly forced uphill towards a cliff of similar proportions to the drop below. Whatever these buildings had been, they had nestled in the angle between two huge cliffs, one rising precipitously before him and the other, hidden by walls, falling sheer to his right. Behind and to the left the ground fell away, tussocky and boulder strewn until it was claimed by the rocks and woods below.

Then from the woods he heard the unmistakable sound of an expletive. Almost certainly Hérault and his men. But for the lucky chance of one of them stumbling and cursing he would have known nothing of them until they had seen him out in the open on this huge step of land, trapped between the cliffs above and the drop to his right. As it was his predicament was almost as bad, with no more than the dubious benefit of a warning. He raced towards the ruins on his right and scrabbled over a pile of stones to fall into dead ground behind them, but with such a clatter of stones that drew a shout from below and an accompanying silencing hiss – presumably from Hérault.

Scanlon froze and listened. For some moments he heard nothing and then began to pick out occasional clicks and scrapings of feet on stones. He lay against a wall at the foot of a slope of fallen stones and debris. To stand, or raise himself at all, would be to expose him to anyone looking up the slope. The wall rose steadily up to the cliff above. If he followed it, even crouching, he would be forced into their line of sight. He toyed with the idea of making a break for it. If he could gain the woods he might evade capture and flee back downhill. It was tempting, but the fear of being cut off was greater.

He examined his immediate surroundings. The wall was solid and overgrown with ryegrass and plantains. Brambles hung over the top. Set into the smaller dry stone courses was a solid vertical stone like a gatepost, against which the scree of rubble he had slid down pressed like a buttress. It extended about six feet from the wall and, although this slope hid him for the time being, it was only a matter of time before he was found. He could not run and he could not stay – could he bargain?

He no longer had the stone but was convinced that it held the key to these bizarre and horrific events. He had assumed that it was Hérault's intention to possess it by any means, but did he know that for certain? Hérault had not actually mentioned it, or anything else specifically, only an unhealthy dislike for Anselm. Perhaps he did not know of it, or its powers. If so, it must still be in St Anselm's.

What had Hérault said after they had brought him round outside St Anselm's? 'The monastery would not reveal its secrets so perhaps it is here. Perhaps that is why he took its name.' Why had 'Anselm' adopted the name from St Anselm's? Why adopt any name at all? Hérault had called him Stephen, and if that was his name why not use it? Perhaps because he had given up his old name in the monastery and, as he had said, he did not feel he could use his monastic name, but why not? And was the Namestone so called because in some way it took the place of a name?

Something hardened inside him. Whatever the mysteries, whatever he did not understand, he knew that he could not betray the Namestone. Somehow he felt it would not permit it anyway.

He was interrupted in his thoughts by the sound of voices at a distance. They had heard him fall but apparently had not seen him. The sounds were from lower down the slope. If they were still searching there he might make a break for it and run to where the ground below the upper cliff sloped down to the woods, meeting it and the cliff together in a tangle of scrub and small trees. It would be a downhill run at right angles to their approach and, although they would have less distance to cross than he had, it would be uphill for them and downhill for him. He might just do it.

He cautiously pulled himself up the rubble to gain a vantage point. Laying flat, he inched up the slope, pulling on the larger stones and slowly raising himself up onto his knees as he approached the top. Well down the slope he saw the weasel-faced Fenster with his back to him and Hérault further down the slope, coming up. It was the perfect moment. He pushed himself up to run but the boulder under his hand fell away into a hollow in the wall and he pitched forward, his arm following the rock up to his shoulder. His left knee was driven into his armpit and jammed his shoulder into the rocks with an excruciating pain. He could not move. Gritting his teeth in a rictus like a maniacal grin, he forced his left knee down onto the rocks so as to drive his upper body up and away from the hole. Instead, the rocks gave way and fell into the hollow beneath. He collapsed onto his chest with his left leg and arm dangling into a drop; only his right arm and leg prevented him from falling in, and it took all his strength to pull himself up enough to free his left arm to brace it against the ruinous wall. He was conscious of a burning pain in his chest, and flung himself over onto his right side. He rolled onto his back and continued onto his front, then threw himself back onto his feet. He found himself looking down the slope to the two men who were running up towards him.

He had lost too much time but they were running up alongside the wall. He could still make it with luck. Leaping out from the top of the slope he launched himself safely and fled downhill at right angles to them. Forty yards and he would gain the woods.

Thirty…

Twenty… he dare not look back.

Ten yards – and he came to a full halt. Out of the woods in front of him stepped the third member of the gang, obviously placed there to foil just such a break as he was making.

Scanlon turned and saw Hérault and Fenster bearing down on him and now also running downhill. Ludicrously for a moment he saw the whole thing resembling a playground game of chase in which the number of chasers grew and grew until just one lone runner remained uncaught. He had been good at that and was often the last one uncaught. In a moment of exhilaration he used his old tactic. Instead of running away from his pursuers he ran towards the gap between them. They turned in towards him but he got through. Their downhill momentum gave him another few yards start and he headed diagonally for the woods down to his right, only to find the heavyweight Harpin running parallel to him, always there to block him while Hérault and Fenster closed in behind.

In desperation Scanlon ran to the wall above the drop. Fenster snatched at his arm and missed. Scanlon leaped up onto the wall and turned, using it as a kicking block to throw himself to the side, falling onto its top along its length. Fenster also leaped up onto the wall and saw the drop below for the first time. His momentum tipped him forwards and in panic Scanlon kicked at his legs. With something between a scream and a gasp of horror he went over the edge, carried outward by his own momentum into a parody of a dive. Scanlon rolled off the wall and lashed out at Hérault coming up behind.

Hérault stood back. 'Don't be a fool, Scanlon. You're going nowhere!'

Scanlon side-stepped but was pinioned by the mountainous brute Harpin, who crashed him back against the wall, pulled him forward and crashed him back again and again.

'Stop!' Hérault shouted the order but the brute turned.

'Stay out of this. This one's mine!' He seized Scanlon by the throat and lifted him bodily onto the wall. 'Thought you were clever, did you? Well, you're going to join him! After I've taught you a lesson.' He lifted Scanlon again and brought his head down onto the stones.

'How does it feel, eh? I'm gonna bounce you on these rocks and then you can bounce down there. You'll be glad to go!'

Hérault said quietly, 'I said stop. We need him.'

'I'll show you how much you need him.' He pushed Scanlon further out over the wall and butted his forehead down onto his face. Scanlon saw him sneer and pull his head back, his eyes fixed callously onto his own. There was blood in Scanlon's eyes. There was a strange sound and for a while nothing happened, until the hideous grin gave way to a puzzled frown. Blood spread on his forehead, and the monster collapsed heavily on top of him.

What felt like an eternity of seconds passed, and Scanlon struggled to free himself. He pulled himself out from under the lifeless body of Harpin and slid off the wall into a sitting position. He blinked and wiped the blood from his eyes and found himself staring into the barrel of a gun.

'As I said, Scanlon, don't be a fool. You're going nowhere.'

Hérault pushed Harpin's body. It slid off the wall and followed Fenster. Scanlon heard the crash and scatter of stones as it hit far below.

'All this foolish effort, Scanlon, all this running – what does it achieve?' Hérault faced him and held the gun casually, but pointing steadily at Scanlon's upper body. Scanlon felt too exhausted to move, in any case.

'A little help; answers to just a few questions. That is all I want. Then I shall not stop you leaving if you wish.'

'You killed Anselm.'

'Harpin killed Anselm. He was without any sense of self-control. He would have killed you if I had not put a stop to him.'

'You gave the orders.'

'And he ignored them, as you saw. I have just saved your life, Scanlon.'

'For some purpose of your own, no doubt.'

'Is that so bad? If my purposes fit with saving your life they cannot be too objectionable. I just need a little reciprocal help in the most minor of matters. For instance, why did you come up here instead of making your escape? What is there here that I have spent so much time searching for, yet have not found? And what – is this?'

With a shock Scanlon watched him draw the Namestone from his pocket. 'Where did you get that?' he exclaimed.

'Oh! So it is important, then? So why did you leave it behind?'

'It is – was – Anselm's – why did you kill him?'

'I have already told you, Harpin killed him. Like you, "Anselm" was more important to me alive than dead, but sometimes these things go wrong. So what is special about this stone? Did it have some special meaning for him? What can you tell me about it?'

'Nothing. It's just a stone. Perhaps it had some sentimental value. If I'm so useful to you alive, why are you pointing a gun at me?'

'Don't underestimate me, Scanlon. This pretty toy can do more than merely kill. It took me a very little time to master its use but I find I can choose to maim or kill with it equally well, and in your case I am prepared to do first one and then the other. Now – sit back and let's talk awhile. What were you looking for up there? Why did you come here? I don't know how you got out but St Anselm's was downhill of Harpin so how did you get by him? And why did you make such an effort to flee uphill? And having done so, how did you know the way to this place?'

Hérault looked at him steadily as he spoke, his face a mask, his eyes half closed. Scanlon could give no answers. He did not know himself how he came to get out of St Anselm's, let alone find himself uphill beyond its guard. If he could not explain that, how could he put his arrival here down to mere accident? He looked around. He recognised now the outlines of the ruins as those of an old monastery – doubtless that which Anselm had described. But its mossy overgrown appearance belied much of what Anselm had said. This ruin – this ruination – was centuries old. How could Anselm and Hérault have stayed here as novices? He found he could not even frame the questions, so how could he either give or evade the answers?

He looked back at Hérault and the gun. Could he see him as a monk? And what of the gun? What had he said? '*It took me a very little time to master it…*' He had spoken as though it had been a novelty to him. '*This pretty toy*', he had called it.

61

Something in this reminded him of Anselm's questioning on their first night – he had asked what year it was! Scanlon's mind screamed a refusal to think this out. He looked at the stone and again a whole miasma of conflicting emotions and perplexities shook him. Involuntarily, he rose to his feet and staggered forwards.

Dimly he heard Hérault shout his name, vaguely saw him raise the gun; the end of the gun was a perfect circle. He froze, half-aware of a mixture of extreme sounds that his brain seemed too over-taxed to sort out from his inner turmoil.

'I said, is this the way over to Alain Pastures?' The question seemed to come from nowhere – totally irrelevantly. Hérault's face looked as baffled as Scanlon felt.

'Alain Pastures? Is this the way?'

'What?' He found himself looking at a small group of hikers who seemed to have appeared from nowhere. Their self-appointed spokesman was obviously waiting for an answer.

'Yes,' Hérault snapped, 'straight downhill through the woods. You will pick up the path as long as you go directly down.' He had lowered the gun into the folds of his jacket.

Scanlon's mind cleared with this sudden absurd intrusion of normality, and he seized the moment. 'Yes, straight down. I'll show you: it's on my way.'

'No, Scanlon,' Hérault said, slightly too loudly. 'We are going the other way.'

There was the shortest of pauses in which Scanlon saw Hérault's hand move briefly to his pocket as his eyes simultaneously scanned the group. Too many, and he had used one bullet already. His hand dropped.

Scanlon breathed again. 'No – I said I could only come with you to the ruins. I'm expected back. You know your way now.' And he moved through the group.

'Follow me. I'll show you,' he waved, smiling to Hérault, 'Cheerio!'

Together, he and the hikers moved downhill, leaving Hérault staring after them with a face like thunder.

'What has happened to you?' asked the spokesman. 'Your face is in quite a state. Have you had a fall?'

'Yes, stupid of me. We were wandering around those ruins and I slipped on a loose heap of stones.'

'Here, I've got some tissues – you need to clean that.' He passed Scanlon a small packet of paper handkerchiefs. 'Strange ruins, aren't they, this old abbey.'

'I think it was a monastery,' said Scanlon.

'Ah yes! St Antipas. It burned down in the sixteenth century.'

'Rebuilt, surely?!'

'No. Apparently it was attacked by robbers and all the monks were killed. The thieves died in the fire but the monastery was never rebuilt.'

They found the path and made time down it. As they passed St Anselm's Scanlon allowed himself only a momentary glance before pressing on steadfastly downhill.

# 10

'A Namestone, you say?' Tim Austin leaned back in his chair.

'That's what he called it.'

They were sitting in Tim's Gloucester flat. Frank had made his way there as soon as he could after his escape the day before. Tim was a friend in need but painstakingly thorough. Frank was making his way through the third retelling of his story. When he had arrived the previous afternoon he had been through several stages of shock and recovery. He was uncharacteristically withdrawn and guarded. It was evident to Tim that something was seriously amiss, but he wisely left it to Frank to broach the subject. Frank chose to collapse into a chair with a huge whisky and brooded undisturbed for some time. Having obtained a promise of a bed for the night he had questioned Tim on local history in a rather dazed and subdued manner that somehow avoided any enquiry on Tim's part. As the evening wore on he became disinclined to make use of the offer of a bed until the whisky took effect. Tim helped him to bed sometime after midnight, and was surprised to find him up before him the next morning, although not in the best of early morning states.

'Frank, do you mind telling me what last night was all about?'

Frank took a deep breath and told Tim the full story for the first time. Having a methodical background Tim asked for a repeat account immediately, then a third. It was not until during the third, quite consistent account, that he made any comment.

The two men went back many years together and held each other in mutual respect. If one had told the other that he had come to believe in fairies, the other would have given the matter a serious consideration that no one else could have commanded.

Tim's interjection about the Namestone did not come at its first appearance in the account. It came when the Namestone was not even part of the story, during Anselm's account of the Sanctuary and his description of the items on the altar. Leaning forward, Tim stared down at his feet. Then he closed his eyes in concentration, as though something at the back of his mind from elsewhere in the story suddenly needed explaining. 'Frank...'

Frank paused and waited. After a while he prompted him. 'Yes, Tim?'

'He called it a Namestone. Whose name, Frank?'

'I don't know. I suppose his – Anselm's.'

'Carry on.'

'Where from?'

'From where you were – the Sanctuary.'

'That was all. The Sanctuary as he described it was in good condition but bare apart from the altar, its furnishings and the lamps. He might have been going to say more about it, although I don't think so, when Hérault arrived.'

'So where is this Namestone now?'

'Hérault has it.'

'But he didn't seem to understand it?'

'No. He said, "Oh! so it is important, then," when he saw my reaction to it. I think that until that moment it was just something he had found in Anselm's room after I'd got out.'

'And you really don't know how you got out?'

'No, except that the Namestone had some part in it.'

Tim was quiet for some time. Then: 'The key to it all is the Sanctuary.'

'How do you know?'

'It has to be, Frank – the Namestone was given to Anselm because of something to do with the monastery. Everything revolves around the monastery, and the monastery revolves around the Sanctuary relics.'

'But they were nothing – a broken jar and a cloth or towel.'

'The jar had hairs on its neck – what colour were they?'

'He didn't say.'

'He said they should have been cleaned off.'

'He said he thought so at the time.'

'What do you mean?'

'I don't know exactly – I got the impression he no longer thought that. There was hardly any time for anything more than impressions – Hérault arrived.'

'Just think, Frank, a monastery guards a precious relic and it has hairs on it that no one cleans off. Why would that be?'

'Because the hairs are part of the relic?'

'Perhaps the most important part!'

'What are you getting at, Tim?'

'I don't know quite – that is – the only thing I can think of is quite incredible. Then there is the towel... she didn't *have* a towel...'

'Who didn't, Tim? What are you getting from this?'

'I don't know... I would like to know whose towel it was. I'm afraid there is only one way to find out. We must return to the monastery.'

'That is impossible! Hérault—'

'He is hardly likely to have remained there. But if he has, then the stone is also there. That is the most remarkable relic of all, although I suspect the term "relic" doesn't apply.'

They discussed the matter of the three bodies and Scanlon's failure to go immediately to the police. 'And tell them that there was a mediaeval monk at St Anselm's who was murdered by another mediaeval monk who had two henchmen that are also dead – one of whom I killed myself? I would have been clapped into the nearest secure psychiatric wing! I'm surprised you believe me.'

'There are levels of belief. Currently I am in danger of believing far more rather than less than you have told me. Right at the start, when you were talking to Anselm about the stone and its properties, you suggested a competent scientist might be able to analyse it, and he agreed?'

'Not quite. He said, *"Perhaps one could"*.'

# 11

They stood outside the locked door of St Anselm's. Tim looked at it steadily, then stepped back and turned away. They had given it one more day, partly to prepare themselves and partly to give Hérault time to be gone. Tim remained standing for some time. Finally he turned and walked to the bench. They sat down.

'If Anselm accepted that a scientist might be able to analyse it, do you mind if this one tries?'

'I wish you would, but it is out of our reach now.'

'Perhaps, perhaps not. If it is what I suspect then it is not far away at all – if distance means anything. It appears to be a stone, it looks hard and greyish – slightly dusty?'

'But it isn't dusty.'

'No, but it looks it. It looks like a grey, dusty stone. It has immense inertia, enough to make you feel as if it draws you, even the earth, to it rather than the other way around.'

'Yes, and it holds visions or aspects of time and place within it that should be inaccessible to you. "The entirety of things past and present," I think you said.'

'Anselm said that. I think he said "the totality". I assume it's the same thing.'

'Same enough: entire, total, they are rather absolutes.' Tim leaned back and stared up at the sky, 'Big – mind-bogglingly big.'

Frank smiled at the *Hitchhiker's Guide* quote. 'It wasn't that big.'

After a while Tim continued, 'What did it weigh, Frank?'

'The Namestone?'

'Could you judge its weight in your hand?'

'No, it had inertia rather than weight. It just is. Somehow it seemed to be the centre of things.'

'Frank, either you are off your rocker or the world is madder than I thought and you are just relatively nuts.'

'Can't help, I'm afraid.'

'Just for the sake of argument, let's assume you are sane and let's try and think this one out. We have a stone that can call to you and in which you can see visions – views of distant places and possibly distant times; times and places that would otherwise be inaccessible to you. It has immense inertia, a centrality that makes everything else seem relative to it. "Everything" is a serious word. Just how all-embracing is your "everything"?'

Scanlon thought for a time before answering. 'I think it is total. I felt as though everything was drawn to it – the earth, the sky, everything.'

'The earth and sky?' Tim paused thoughtfully. 'You really felt that?'

'Yes, there was a sense of complete shift. It had a greater reality; everything else seemed relative to it.'

'Seemed?'

'No, that's too weak. I am sure that everything *was* relative to it. It is a mystery, but I was – am – totally convinced of it.'

Tim leaned forward, looking down and pressing his fingers to his temples. 'There is only one thing that contains the totality of all things past and present. I suppose it is the biggest recording device ever made. As it works entirely on the principle of energy focused at points of action, it could perhaps be focused itself. If so, it might look like a stone.'

Frank waited a few seconds then burst out, 'Look! I've learned lately that life can be far shorter than we think! Isn't it time you stopped being cryptic and said something positive?'

'I'm sorry, it's just that what has happened to you is so strange that any conclusions drawn from it have to be so extreme as to be unbelievable.'

'I suspended belief some time ago.'

'Very well.' Tim took a deep breath. 'Your stone – Anselm's stone – has properties only shared by one thing. The only entity that holds a complete record of all events present and past is the cosmos itself.' He forestalled Frank with a brief gesture.

'By its very nature all events are held within it. Every particle in it is affected by every other particle, and the results of those effects are permanently bound up in a sort of internal harmony. I'm afraid the more I try to explain it the harder it gets to understand, but the bottom line is that you cannot do anything without leaving a record which the universe holds like some great storage medium.'

'But surely I can do something without affecting the entire universe? Look,' Frank fished in his pocket, 'two coins of the same value. If I swap them without you looking you could not tell anything had happened. I could do that with large or small things, even atoms.'

Tim shrugged. 'Electrons would be a better example: all electrons are indistinguishable, but nevertheless, to exchange two takes energy, and that affects neighbouring particles. Furthermore, all particles act as – probably are – no more than the points of action of their wave functions, their energy fields, if you like, and there is no such thing as a localised field. They are infinite.'

'Aren't we getting away from the Namestone here?'

'Not really. You look into the stone as though you are looking into the universe and seeing its history. I'm sorry, I can't come up with anything else.'

'Well, it obviously isn't the universe, and your argument seems self-defeating. If every bit of the universe affects every other, then any bit contains a record of all the rest. The Namestone would be unnecessary.'

'In a way, yes, but it is like a hologram – any bit you break off contains information of the whole picture. You can see the whole picture in it but there is increasing loss of detail as the piece gets smaller. There was no loss of detail in the stone as you described it. It even maintains momentum and inertia. Where were you when you first looked into it?'

Frank led him to the patch of ground where he had lain after helping Anselm with the logs. Tim squatted down and looked left and right. 'And the log store is round there?'

'Yes, you can't see it from here.'

Tim turned and looked towards the path. After a while he got to his feet and walked towards the bench by the door where both he and Frank sat down, with Tim deep in thought. Tim finally broke the silence. 'Never mind, right or wrong, I am sure the answer lies in the monastery Sanctuary.'

'Let's go then.' They turned away from the locked building with its grim secret and found the uphill path.

'Tim, I don't think you realise just what a ruin this place is. There's hardly anything there – no buildings, no chapel, no Sanctuary. Hérault and Fenster searched the ruins for a whole day and found nothing. I've seen it – it's just grass and stones.'

'If that is all there is then it will be a sort of answer, but a disappointing and puzzling one. Do you think you can find your way?'

'I think so. Between Hérault and his crew and me and the ramblers it should be a well-beaten path by now. There's the way to the pool,' he said, pointing right.

They continued uphill in silence for a time until they came to a point where the path bore right. Gaps in the scrub and boot marks on the ground showed a number of people had come and gone straight on. And so, by degrees, they approached the monastery site. They came upon it unexpectedly and had stepped several paces into the open when they saw a seated figure uphill, its back towards them. Scanlon froze. Breaks in the scudding clouds alternately darkened and lit the hillside.

'It's Hérault!'

They stood for a moment, uncertain, but the figure did not move.

'We've got to go back. He's armed!'

'Wait,' said Tim quietly. 'What can he be doing here?'

Scanlon stood, uncertain. Hérault seemed unnaturally still. Surely he must have heard them? As if answering his thoughts Hérault raised his head, still with his back to them, and appeared to stare up the slope. High up towards the cliff face another figure was standing, looking down towards them, momentarily caught in sunlight. A rushing sound filled Scanlon's ears, and his vision contracted to a point as though he was about to pass out. The ground under his feet felt unsteady and false, as though he were standing on water. The noise in his head grew with the insistence of air rushing through an organ pipe. His peripheral vision became a mist but with a central point of absolute clarity. His ears filled with the sound of the stone and his eyes focused beyond Hérault on to the unmistakable face of Anselm!

# 12

Tim's hand gripped his upper arm. 'Steady, Frank! What's happening? Who is that?'

The steadying hand stopped Scanlon from sinking to his knees, and the hillside leapt back into focus. Hérault began to rise to his feet as Anselm walked a few paces down the hill towards them and stopped. Scanlon did not know what to do. He was far from sure that Hérault had any further use for him that would give him any protection, and quite sure that Tim had no protection at all. At any second he expected Hérault to turn, but at the same time he felt that the appearance of Anselm was for the moment at least sufficient distraction.

Hérault stood and walked slowly up the hill.

What was he doing there? It was two days since Scanlon had left, and three since Anselm's… since Anselm had been…

'Tim, he had rigor mortis!'

Hérault checked at Scanlon's voice but did not look back. With the appearance of great weariness he resumed his way uphill towards Anselm. Scanlon moved to follow him, with Tim still holding his arm.

Scanlon looked at Tim. 'Do you hear it?'

'Hear what?'

'The stone.'

'No, nothing, but I am not surprised if you do. Somehow you are essential to all this. I take it that is Anselm?'

'Yes. You must think me mad, but he was dead.'

'I am sure, and at the same time I am sure he was not. He is both dead and alive far more than you have understood.'

'I understood more than I said – he died before I met him.'

'And so he couldn't die again.'

'But his body…'

'This is not the time for discussion. Can you walk on your own?'

'Yes.'

Tim released his arm and they followed Hérault up the slope. For Scanlon alone, the deep diapason of the stone pervaded everything. Once again there was the overwhelming feeling that it was the true reality and everything else just harmonies within it: the rocks; the turf, trees and cliffs; Tim and himself, all seemed to be harmonies within the greater note. Hérault was there, too, of course, but a discord. And Anselm? Scanlon blinked and refocused. Anselm was still there. Somehow Scanlon expected him to disappear like a phantom, but no, he gazed steadily down on the three of them from his place on the upper slope. He was strangely silent. Not that there would be any point in his speaking because they were still too far away, but somehow he seemed to possess a silent stillness, as though he absorbed rather than gave out sound.

The three of them walked steadily uphill. Scanlon recognised the place where Anselm stood as the slope of stones against the wall where he had hidden two days before. Anselm's gaze shifted from one to the other of them as they approached and he took a few more steps down the slope towards them. Even this did not destroy the extraordinary stillness he had – a centrality that the song of the stone and the harmonies that played in it did nothing to disturb.

Hérault stopped about twenty feet from Anselm, with Tim and Scanlon just behind him. Scanlon saw the gun held loose and disregarded in his right hand. After a moment he spoke in a cracked voice somewhere between a sneer and hate.

'Stephen! Death becomes you!' He turned and looked Scanlon in the eyes.

To his horror, Scanlon saw his face for the first time, decimated with sunken cheeks and eyes, and several days' stubble. His lips were cracked and bleeding with spittle at the corners. How had three days brought him to this? 'Send your friend away! He has no business here!'

'Hérault,' Anselm spoke, 'we all have business here. You are searching for a power you can neither control nor understand, for which you have deceived, killed and destroyed, and which would have been freely given you if you only knew how to ask.'

'Ask! You talk of asking? Power does not come by asking; it has to be grasped and used. I despise bringers of gifts – they are weak and only a little less despicable than those who would accept what they offer. I cannot be beholden to you or to any power on earth. What I want I take, and what I cannot take I destroy. That is power!'

Tim heard this but Scanlon heard hardly a word. The sound of the stone in his head had grown to deafening proportions. Hérault's words were no more than a meaningless interference in something that encompassed the whole eminence on which they stood. Something remarkable was unfolding before his eyes. Something intimately involved with the stone, as though the entire hillside was part of it, transformed by it. Everything except Anselm himself. The stone ruins shimmered in the resonance of its call. They remained ruins but at the same time he saw the walls rising like ghosts from the rubble. Tall stone arches, gothic windows constructed into Norman walls rebuilt from Saxon hewn stones, many hewn from other pre-Christian monoliths. The whole area sang the song of the Namestone, and Scanlon felt his whole body drawn into its music. He saw people – monks – moving between the rooms, building, rebuilding, following daily routines of waking and sleeping, worship and housekeeping. Everything had its place in the harmony, himself included. Yet Anselm was strangely different, part and separate at once, like the eye of the storm.

'What is happening? You must tell me what is happening!' Tim whispered urgently beside Scanlon.

'I can see the monastery: the Namestone brings it to life. Its whole history and prehistory. This has been a place of faith long before the coming of Christianity.'

'The stone shows you this? Where is it?'

'This pebble?' Hérault held up the Namestone in his left hand, the gun still hanging loosely in his right. 'It's a stone, a mere stone. I have studied it for days and it is mere stone, a red herring of a stone. But there is something here, something that brings a monk back from the dead – that has brought me, and provided me with powers stronger than anything you can imagine – eh, Anselm? Stephen – Anselm – is that what we call you now, Stephen? Perhaps I should change my name, too. What shall we have? Nemesis? Your fate looms, Anselm. You may have found survival against all nature, but so have I – so have I, and I will take your powers from you or destroy this place along with it.'

He turned on his heel and faced Scanlon. 'Somehow you have seen into this place. It predates Christianity and the pitiful sects and doctrines it produced. There are earth gods here with true power, which drew this superficial scum to it like detritus into a whirlpool. You know this, Scanlon. You can sense it. It is a gift you have, but I have a gift, too – a gift for using knowledge and seizing opportunities. You have a gift in the way a mine has gold, but I have the ability to mine it and use it. I can offer you everything you have ever dreamed of, and more. I can give you revenge on all the petty injustices you have suffered, or, if you wish it, the power to right all the petty wrongs you have ever done. Think of it, Scanlon. You have seen something here, haven't you? You know there is power here. You can't control it, but I can if you let me guide you. And I can show you how to control it.'

Tim, standing a pace behind Scanlon, saw him shake his head, confused; saw him half turn his head away but keep his eyes on Hérault as though threatened, saying nothing.

'Power, Scanlon, the ability to accomplish anything you want,' Hérault continued in an almost hypnotic monotone. 'How did you get out of the lodge, Scanlon? How did you anticipate my arrival? Why have you returned? Why, Scanlon, did you come here in the first place? What were you getting away from?'

Tim saw Scanlon sag. He had a sudden deflated air. His eyes drifted away from Hérault's face and he took a few steps forward. 'Don't listen to him, Frank!'

Hérault turned towards Tim and the gun raised perceptively in his hand. Just an inch or two, but enough to be threatening, and yet at the same time it could have been merely accidental.

'You don't need to listen to me,' Hérault continued in the same monotone. 'You have it all in yourself. But I am an interpreter. If you will let me, I can help you use whatever power you have.'

'Put that damn gun away!' Tim snapped, feeling the almost unbearable tension. Hérault looked vaguely at it as though surprised to find it in his hand, but his almost absent-minded inspection left it pointing directly at Tim, although it was flat in his hand. His finger remained on the trigger.

'Give me the stone,' said Scanlon wearily.

Hérault looked suddenly at him, his grip tightening on the gun and stone together. 'The stone? Is there something in this pebble, after all?'

'Give it to me. I can do nothing without it.' Scanlon's voice was flat and unemotional. Tim was puzzled: nothing that he knew of his friend was conveyed in the dull, lifeless tones of that voice. He looked for the first time at the Namestone. Like Hérault, he saw just a grey pebble that one might pick up on any seaside beach. He could discern neither the dark flecks nor the brightness that his friend had described. Standing as he was he could see Anselm, still motionless but observant, uphill. Scanlon and Hérault were on either side of Tim's line of sight,

Hérault holding the stone half extended in his left hand and the gun in his right, still pointing downhill to Tim on his left. It all resembled some strange set piece – a tableau. Tim wondered how accurate Hérault could be with the gun pointed in this awkward way and was disconcerted to see the barrel was levelled straight at him. Somehow he had ceased to be a mere observer.

Hérault's next words confirmed this. 'I think, Scanlon, that your friend has a little too much interest in these events. You and I have an understanding, but I'm not sure he shares it. If I give you the stone, and if it has any properties that I have not discovered, then you and I together can make full use of them, but I think your friend may have another agenda.' He removed all uncertainty about the gun by half turning to Tim and pointing it directly at him, level and hard. The Namestone remained in his left hand – now clasped tight against his chest.

'Perhaps we should remove him. He is irrelevant. I tire of him.'

Scanlon looked from Hérault to Tim and back again with a blank emptiness about his gaze that made Tim's flesh creep. He wanted to appeal to Anselm but feared that anything he did might literally trigger an unpleasant event. He called out instead to his friend, 'For pity's sake, Frank!'

Scanlon looked back at him. 'I did come here to get away – perhaps to find something. Strange, I had almost forgotten. The Namestone makes the most apparently important things seem peripheral. It gives everything a new centre. From the moment I first saw it there were answers for me. I didn't realise it at first, but what I was searching for was there in its mere mystery, before it ever called me.'

'Frank – pull yourself together. Whatever it is, whatever it possesses, it is not yours. It is not Hérault's; it is Anselm's.'

'Anselm is dead.'

'He is not. He is there on the slope.'

'He is dead.'

'Frank, look at him. Look at him now.'

'I don't need to look. I have looked and I don't believe my eyes. The world's gone mad but there is a thread through its madness. One end is the reason I came out here and the other is the chance to use the madness against itself, perhaps even to destroy it.'

'I don't know what you are talking about. I only know that the stone is neither yours nor Hérault's and should be returned to its owner. This man Hérault is evil!'

'I don't know that. He did save my life!'

'You do know,' Hérault interjected quietly. 'I am evil. I admit it. After all, what is evil? In a mad world it is the chance to reshape everything in a new mould:

"Could thou and I with fate conspire
to grasp this sorry Scheme of Things entire?
Would we not shatter it to bits
– and then remould it nearer to the Heart's Desire!"

'Throw out the old and make it anew – our way?'

'Your way!' Tim rounded on him. 'Your way is destruction. Everything sacrificed to your ends. You would kill to get what you want – no doubt you saved Frank's life to get what you want. It suited your purpose at the time, and when it no longer suited you, you would kill as soon as not.'

'Perhaps, but at least others have the chance to do the same. Isn't that so, Scanlon? Aren't there things you want to change? One thing in particular, perhaps?'

'Don't listen to him, Frank!'

'There is one thing. The reason I came out here on my own. I had to sort myself out and needed solitude.'

'Frank, we have known each other for more years than I can remember. We have faced more together than most friends; we know each other well; we share the same sense of right and wrong. How can you listen to this megalomaniac?'

'Our friendship was coming to an end anyway, Tim.'

'How?'

'Death,' said Hérault. 'There is death in the air. I can smell it. That's right, isn't it, Scanlon?'

'Yes. Maybe not soon, but inevitably. I am dying. I learned it before I set out on this – this – holiday.' He grimaced. Tim found himself unable to speak. Scanlon went on, 'If I'm to take the doctors' word for it, which I suppose I must. So you see, Tim, everything was coming to an end anyway. The world was changed for me before all this happened, and where before my life had been the centre of things, my death suddenly took its place. Then just as suddenly the Namestone changed everything again. That and—' he glanced quickly at Hérault, then uphill towards Anselm. 'Don't you see, Tim?' he said suddenly. 'There is something momentous here. This monastery, it is a mediaeval ruin and yet Anselm knew it well. He and Hérault stayed here, trained as monks here...' he gestured helplessly at the ruins.

A sudden flurry of raindrops was followed by a brief lifting of the clouds, and then the lower slope darkened again.

'There is survival here.' He turned away from Tim towards Hérault. 'Give me the stone.'

Hérault eyed him thoughtfully and then looked down at the stone in his hand. 'You called it a Namestone. Do you understand what that means?'

'I don't know. That is what Anselm called it.'

'Did he now? He seems, however, to be very confused about names. I knew him as Simon, but when he became a monk he was given the name of Stephen, and now he is Anselm.'

'He never mentioned the name Simon.'

'For goodness sake you two!' Tim burst out. 'While you discuss his property and his name he is standing here with us. Why don't you ask him what all this means?'

'A reasonable request!' Hérault held out the stone. 'Perhaps you can persuade him to help us.'

Tim took the stone and strode past them up the hill. He had scarcely gone ten paces when Hérault, with an almost casual air, raised the gun and fired.

# 13

Tim stiffened and stopped in his tracks. He dropped slowly to his knees, still looking at Anselm. Even more slowly he settled back onto his heels and Scanlon saw a blood-stained hole in the back of his jacket. He saw Anselm raise his hand. The world seemed to come to a stop. Someone was shouting; he heard a screamed 'NO!' and incoherent shouts of rage. He found himself grasping the gun by the barrel with one hand and Hérault by the throat with the other. The cries of rage went on. As he drove the gun up into Hérault's face he realised he was making them himself. Hérault still held the gun by the butt, but made no resistance. He thrust the gun rapidly into Hérault's face three times and sank the fingers of his right hand into his throat. Wrenching the gun from his grasp he transferred it to his right hand and levelled it at Hérault's head.

Blood thundered in his veins and coloured his vision red. Everything seemed red except Hérault. Hérault was a dark menace. Scanlon blinked, confused. Something was happening to his vision. It pulsated red, and again that deep, penetrating note filled him and the world about him. As before, it commanded and compelled, but there was a difference. He felt a resonance like that of the stone-call with the stones under his feet and the gun in his hand. He saw it in his reddening vision, heard and felt it crashing in unison with his blood, his breath and his inarticulate sobs. But he also saw it in Hérault's face, resonating with the black of his pupils, the caverns of his nostrils and mouth, the blackness of his hair.

The whole situation was foul and unnatural. Hérault emanated evil. Tim was dead or dying; Anselm was both dead and alive, or something worse, and overriding all of this, overriding his hate and his hand on the gun, was some deeper wrong beyond his understanding. The redness of his vision picked out elements of the scene like a pervasive colour in a pattern. These elements were not red; they were black. Dark with excess of red. Hérault's face was a dark leer.

'Dark with excess of red.'

As a boy he had read of the throne of God as 'dark with excessive bright'. Some far memory of that phrase was echoed here as a terrible negative of the throne of God. The loom of Hérault's face swallowed everything; growing, unnerving his mind and sinews. He was undone. He made to let the gun drop. His knees buckled and lowered him to the ground, but the gun did not drop. The focus of this horror destroyed all his self-control. He had no power of himself to help himself, his limbs would not work and his bowels would not hold. He could not even make a voluntary breath. Vomit was in his throat; and yet the gun did not drop.

The sound held his hand on the gun and kept it raised, and though it shuddered through his body it did not suffer his fingers to release it. He could not move his fingers but felt, more through the sound than through his senses, that the gun was positively directed. He tried to look down but found his eyes frozen on Hérault's face.

It broke into an abyss of a grin. His mouth opened in a maelstrom of darkness, his teeth blackly red. The crescendo of sound screamed, no longer a resonance of some cosmic harmony but an unutterable disharmony of sound, light and the foul stench of his breath.

Suddenly he was released and fell back onto his heels. His mind filled with the pitiful picture of Tim collapsing with a flowing bullet wound in his back. His eyes broke away from Hérault's face as though a string had snapped. His chin dropped to his chest and he found himself looking down at the gun. It was not pointed at Hérault. Its muzzle was a black hole pointed directly at his eyes. It was in his hand but he had no power to move it.

'Scanlon, you miserable wretch. You are mine, more than you know. Look at that black hole. Do you know what it is?'

Scanlon's vocal chords echoed his thoughts, but without his volition. 'A gun barrel.'

'No, Scanlon, it is a way out. A gateway to eternal life, but not happily ever after, Scanlon. No, not happily ever after.'

The end of the barrel swelled in Scanlon's vision; its black cavern beckoned red.

'Happiness is not for you or me, Scanlon. Where would we find happiness in this dark, tortured world? Satisfaction, perhaps; not happiness. Satiety comes through power, Scanlon. I have power and I will give a little to you. Yes, I think just a little – enough to squeeze the trigger. Think what that little power can bring you. Oblivion? Escape? Perhaps far more. I can permit you a few answers. You are Scanlon; I am Hérault; Anselm – Stephen – Simon – perhaps he is working his way through all the names in the book, but each of us, Scanlon, has an animus and a corpus, some unity of body and soul, greater than the here and now of your petty life.

'You think you are dying. Perhaps you are, but you need not. I can offer you survival and power. Power beyond your imagining, but you must make the step yourself. Stand up. Look about you. Tell me what you see.'

Scanlon felt a tiny release. He stood, his head and eyes turned, but still with the sense of happening without his volition. He saw again the ghost-walls of the old monastery, more solid than before. Anselm and Tim were nowhere to be seen. He was standing in a broad colonnade which ran around a paved courtyard.

'What do you see?'

He looked around at the sound of Hérault's voice, but he was alone. Startled, he blinked and turned and almost fell. At once the scene changed back to the monastery ruins. Hérault was standing as before, regarding him.

'What did you see?' the question was snapped and peremptory. Scanlon was too confused to answer.

'What did you see?' Hérault repeated in a sharper pitch.

Something in the tone of his question jarred in Scanlon's mind. He still felt powerless but the raised pitch of interrogation interfered with the intensity of Hérault's control. He looked around. Again he saw the ghost-walls superimposed on the scene around him, but faint and confused as in a delirium. Hérault took a step towards him. 'Scanlon! Hear me! You have the power to turn this all to account, the power to seize power, but what I have is greater. I have the power to control, given to me in a manner you cannot imagine, but it is mine to use and to share. Obey me and unimagined power and riches will be yours. Disobey me at your peril!'

With the word 'disobey', a shock of pain arched Scanlon's back as though his whole body had been drilled through by a bolt of electricity. Blue fire flashed in his vision. The gun dropped unnoticed from his nerveless fingers and the pain rolled and cracked through his limbs like an aftershock. He found himself on his knees again and fell forwards onto his hands.

'Get up!' He felt himself being hauled to his feet. The discordant sound racked through him again, and with it the monastery ruins began to rebuild themselves.

'What can you see?'

'The monastery.'

'Describe it.'

'The walls are complete – not ruins.'

'Describe it.'

'We are in a cloister – with stone columns – square columns around a courtyard.'

'Describe the courtyard.'

'It's square. I can't see it well; it's dark.'

'Dark?'

'Yes, evening.' The scene took fuller form again as he peered into it. He was looking between two solid pillars of stone out across a flagged courtyard in the late evening. He looked carefully round, so as not to break the vision. The dark colonnade stretched behind him. He could not see Hérault; he did not expect to. Hérault belonged to the other world; too much attention to him or to it would drag him back there. He could still hear the sounds of Hérault, his breath and movements. He heard a thrush singing, but his eyes saw the gathering night in an ancient cloister.

'What is the courtyard like? Grass? Gravel?' Hérault's voice grated on his consciousness.

'Flagstones. It is paved with flagstones.'

'Yes, it was flagstones; you couldn't have known that. You could not have known. You are really seeing it.' He was quiet for some seconds; the seconds stretched interminably. Scanlon felt unbelievably tired and weak, gripped by a great inertia. Once more he looked slowly about him. A sudden movement or deliberate effort would break the spell. Somehow he felt safer in the cloister, except he was not sure that he was in the cloister. Perhaps he was standing in front of Hérault in bright daylight; perhaps he was standing in the cloister at night: his ears told him one thing; his eyes another. How was he seeing the courtyard anyway? He did not have the stone, did not even know what had become of it. He tried to listen to the name-sound but felt only discord.

He stared into the dark. Darkness swam against darkness. Shadows filled his mind with grotesque imaginings, clouds covered the moon, blackness filled the colonnade, column shadows merged with dark surrounding walls; the courtyard by comparison was a miasma of mere gloom. Still Scanlon strained to hear the name-sound as the seconds stretched into eternity and eternity folded back on itself into seconds. Was this a Namestone image or something conjured up by Hérault?

He did not know. He felt safer where he was, but was that an illusion? There was only one way to find out. He broke the link and found himself staring into Hérault's face.

There was blood on Hérault's lip where he had driven the gun into it. Hérault held the gun again. Scanlon looked around, blinking in the sunlight. Where were Anselm and Tim? They were no more here than they had been in the courtyard. He looked back into Hérault's face and struggled against the enervating tiredness. Fighting for words he gasped, 'You will not control me!'

At once he was lashed with pain, but something in the pitch of Hérault's anger interfered with his control. 'Where is Tim? Why do you need me to see the old monastery? What has it to do with you and with Anselm? For heaven's sake, what are you? Some sort of demon? Will you kill me as well? If you are so convinced I can lead you to some source of power, what good would it do to kill me?' Questions poured out of Scanlon almost too fast for him to take a breath. Hérault raised the gun, and Scanlon waited.

'Yes, you are right: it will do me no good to kill you now.' He seemed to have reached some level of composure and regarded Scanlon thoughtfully. 'Am I a demon? I wonder – certainly not for heaven's sake anyway. Do we know what a demon is, or what can become one? Demons have power over mere human animals certainly, as I have power over you, but if I am a demon it is a status I have earned. I serve a greater master.'

'Or a lower one!'

'Don't play with me, Scanlon! The game is too deep for you! Come with me; there is nothing to be gained here.'

He strode across the grass slope to the stone-lidded trough and fallen columns where Scanlon had slept the first time he came to the ruins. Scanlon followed, wondering. Standing before what he had previously taken to be some sort of large cistern, he made out the worn remains of carvings on the stone. One of the pillars appeared to have fallen over, and in various places stones had been moved and the earth disturbed. 'What is this?' Scanlon asked.

Hérault regarded him strangely. 'You should be able to tell me, Scanlon. You have an ability to see what is really here, not just the artefacts of the present. I believe you do not understand your power, but somehow you use it, or it uses you. I need to know the source of your ability. And you – you, Scanlon! – your needs and desires closely match mine – more than you know. You think I have power over you, and I have, but only because deep down your hopes and desires, your pain, matches mine! I know you, Scanlon, better than you know yourself. You fight me out of your hatred and out of your desire. You fight me to master me. I am stronger than you, but deep inside you is a knot of hunger, thirst and loss which drives you. I know it well. It is the shriek of the damned, Scanlon! The sharpened recognition of betrayal – of finding God turned Judas; the discovery that there is no home for you in this universe unless you can force it to your will against all opposition, against God, against everything that would destroy you, and against me! You and I are one and the same, Scanlon; the only alternative we have is destruction, but the goal is ultimate power: for you, power over the disease that rots you from inside; for me, power over the petty fools I am forced to share this universe with. We may be incompatible, you and I, but at the moment we need each other; we each have something the other wants, and, for the moment, it makes sense to work together.'

'You have nothing I want!'

Hérault made no reply. He stood, piercing Scanlon with a fixed stare. Scanlon's vision wavered. Hérault remained clear but all around him became dark, indistinct and filled with vague motion. The sky looked black above and behind him, and clouds whirled and coalesced in a gathering storm.

Everything in his vision, other than Hérault himself, gathered into the menacing shadow of a vast creature against which Hérault stood outlined. Black wings blotted out the sky, lightning flickered in its eyes, lurid light played in its gaping maw. Hérault raised his right arm and appeared to draw darkness out of the sky. Slowly he brought his arm down before him and pointed at Scanlon's chest. An indistinct cloud, stained with a blood-red hue, poured from his hand and Scanlon felt it flooding into him. He braced himself but there was no pain, just a skittering on his chest like a hundred cobwebbed insects before which his own pain, the pain that he had carried with him for the past months, shrank and faded as though anaesthetised.

The earth throbbed under his feet once, and then all was still. He stood alone on the hillside with Hérault beside the cistern. His tiredness was gone, and the accompanying pain with it. He looked about him at the clearing sky and took a deep breath. His lungs expanded freely for the first time in months.

He stepped towards the cistern and felt in control, balanced, like an athlete. Looking towards Hérault he was momentarily taken aback: every pore, every hair of the man was seen with an awful clarity. What was it that was so disturbing? He looked at the carvings on the rock, at the sky, at the ruined walls and at the man. That same disturbing clarity enhanced them all. He examined his own hands and saw the same – every pore, every crease, every particle of dirt sharp and distinct – yet something was wrong. What was it? The clarity had startled him, but his vision had always been good, so why should this seem so unusual? A fragment of verse came to mind:

> There follows a mist and a weeping rain,
> And life is never the same again.'

But what had changed?

'Brings things into focus, doesn't it?' said Hérault, 'Now you see things as they really are. I know – I have been there, stood in your shoes and seen what you see – long, long ago.'

'What have you done? What was that behind you? The greater master you say you serve?'

'You have much to learn, Scanlon. For now it is enough that you know what power is at our disposal. Feeling better, eh?'

'Yes – I mean no – something is missing.'

'That is what we are here to find.'

'No you are wrong – something has gone – been taken from me.'

'Never mind, I need you to see the monastery as it was. Something is hidden here and you can help me find it.'

'Why should I help you?'

'Don't you feel what has happened to you? I have control over your diseased body, Scanlon. I can return the pain as easily as I took it away. Do you feel stronger? Where do you think that strength comes from? From me, Scanlon! And do you think I am some disinterested, benevolent benefactor? Your only hope is to seize the force this monastery holds – and I think that perhaps you know more about that than you told me. Well! We shall see!'

Scanlon felt again the resonance of command. The ghost-walls of the monastery pulsated with its call. The night scene throbbed in his vision with a discordant crescendo. The sound was powerful, martial, deep, almost below the level of hearing but palpable, striking both mind and body with compulsion to obey. He responded, and felt that he was part of it.

From somewhere else he also heard a second call, deeper and harmonic – not pulsating, but it was faint, or perhaps he thrust it to the back of his mind. The martial discord was bringing the scene to life before him and helping him leave Hérault behind. He stood again at the edge of the deserted courtyard. Although it was dark, there were lights in a few windows and in a half-open doorway away to his left. He tried to move towards it as he had moved when he first used the stone, but nothing happened. He looked down at his feet and saw them planted squarely on the cobbles of the colonnade, although they felt as though they were on grass. Taking a tentative step he felt the grass brush his ankles, even though his eyes told him there were cobbles.

He peered down and for a moment caught the glint of sunlight on stems, but seen through the dark filter of the evening courtyard.

'Well?' said Hérault's voice. Instinctively he straightened and shut out both the sun and the voice. He walked on, ignoring the incongruous brushing at his feet. Crossing the courtyard, he approached the lit doorway. As he did so he was struck again by the unnatural clarity of the scene. Unnatural? Perhaps not; unpleasant, certainly, but if anything intensely natural, as though every particle of reality was acutely emphasised. And yet, just as in the ruined, sunlit scene with Hérault, there was a sense of loss and deprivation. He drew near the door, skirting a column. Another query came from Hérault but he made himself ignore it. Reaching the door he peered cautiously inside and found himself staring into the monastery chapel. A man stood with his back to him, dressed in a coarse monkish habit.

Again he heard Hérault's voice following close behind. Scanlon felt his mind must break under one conflict too many. As soon as he entered the doorway the vibrant, martial resonance that seemed to call the scene into being rose until his ears hurt. The sound of Hérault behind him echoed within it like noises in a cavern, but instead of dying the echo grew, and as it grew the discord grew with it. Hérault's actual words were drowned out, but the sense was unmistakable. Scanlon was being both commanded and threatened. He was being told over and again to report what he saw, but the pain in his ears was oppressive. To reply would only add to the cacophony and the pain. His knees sagged.

Simultaneously he was aware of the second call that he had been suppressing at the edge of his consciousness. A deeper, quieter persistence, not heard through the ears but resonating in and through everything. It competed with nothing, not even with the discord through which the monastery appeared to be conjured into being. It brought no pain but it was a distraction that threatened his control of the vision, and if he lost that he would be back in the daylit ruins at the mercy of Hérault. Nevertheless, there in the doorway, as he stared at the back of the standing figure, it grew, and growing, called more strongly. The man before him was looking this way and that. Even from the back a familiar figure can be recognised. The two competing calls grew – one summoning and holding the scene with a stark but aweful clarity, the other resonating and underlying with a deeper indefinable quality. Part of him was torn between them, while another looked on in wonder and fear.

The figure turned and fear won. As Hérault's threatening voice behind forced him to his knees demanding that he tell what he saw, he stared up into Hérault's face lit by the chapel lamps!

Scanlon felt trapped. A mediaeval Hérault stood facing him in the doorway, while the twentieth century Hérault cajoled and threatened from behind. He found himself frozen in a crouching attitude on the ground, just as many years ago he had frozen on a rock face. On that occasion he had recalled stories of climbers who had lost their nerve and clung until their fingers could no longer hold and they fell to their deaths. As he stared into Hérault's face in the chapel he saw no flicker of recognition. The man looked straight through him. Still Scanlon could not move; the absolute impossibility he was facing left him totally unnerved. Everything was suspended in one impossible moment.

Breathing! Breathing was the one control he had left. On the rock face he had used this to break the spell. By controlling his breathing he had controlled his terror. Scanlon breathed slowly out, stilling the urge to pant. His eyes remained fixed on the mediaeval Hérault's face, waiting for him to make a move. Beyond him another man moved steadily across the chapel, staring down at the floor as though searching, his eyes flicking from left to right. Hérault continued to stare fixedly through Scanlon. Scanlon breathed deeply and rocked back onto his heels, rising slightly.

'Scanlon! What are you seeing?' Hérault's voice came again from behind, but the figure before him remained still. Frank stiffened as a hand descended on his shoulder. Still the figure before him stared down, but no longer directly at him. He had moved sufficiently to be out of the line of gaze, and the eyes had not followed him. The Hérault he could see could not see him! The hand on his shoulder gripped painfully and shook him. His freeze broke. Involuntarily he looked round and found himself again staring into Hérault's face, but this time there was no doubt that he was seen.

'Speak to me, man! What are you seeing?'

Still he could not answer. The sheer implausibility of what he was seeing struck him dumb, forcing him into the role of a bewildered, passive observer. Hérault mouthed unheard words at him, demanding, accusing, threatening. He stared back, confused; the ancient walls had again melted away. He felt himself struck, once, twice – he felt he should be angry, respond, protest, strike back, but did none of those things. There was nothing to be gained here. Somehow he had to make sense of this, and the Hérault before him was losing control in an outburst of anger.

Scanlon retreated into himself. The discord that had called the ancient monastery into being was still there, but Hérault's anger was disrupting it, and underneath he could again discern that sustaining, undemanding harmony, the call of the Namestone. He had known it for that all along, even when pushing it out of his mind. He also knew he had failed in this. The name-sound had been the one constant in all this madness, though not compelling – Anselm had said it could compel but he had not found it so here. Indeed, he felt it offered him the choice either to accept or reject it, but he knew he had nowhere else to go. The fearsome, particular clarity of the scene Hérault had thrust him into was terrifying in its awful reality, but in spite of its stark clarity it carried an implacable sense of loss. The name-sound was altogether complete, absolute, central and all-embracing, the only fixed point of reference in this mad affair.

# 14

## The monastery, 1594

Barnabas was stirring feverishly in the infirmary, tended by one of the younger brothers, and in his absence his Keeper's vigil in the Sanctuary was taken by Stephen. Stephen had entered the Sanctuary some hours before Vespers in the early evening, relieving Phillip, who had flexed his stiffened muscles, bowed in silence and retreated reverently to the steps where he made a deep genuflection as though to a High Altar, turned and left. Moments later Stephen heard the Sanctuary stone close above him. He was already in prayer.

In the solitude of the Sanctuary vigil one became aware of the dark and the light to an enhanced degree. He was used to this. The black stones of the wall cast blacker shadows beneath, against which the lanterns stood out as bright islands of flame. It had to be an illusion, perhaps caused by the relative brightness of the reliquary table, but the light seemed to stream from the lamps to the table with nothing reflected back to relieve the darkness of the walls. They seemed to convey a dark cloak in which the relics on the table shone unquenched.

The flaming torches and the illuminated table with its brighter relics shone in the darkness which forever seemed about to close in and snuff them out, and forever failed. All this Stephen was used to. It had been a part of every vigil since he had become a Keeper. Each vigil had become an increasing struggle, a fight between light and dark, both within himself and in the Sanctuary. This time, however, the perspective seemed to be reversed. The tension between dark and light was enhanced, but the light was different. It took some time to pin down just what it was. Everything looked the same and yet he felt lost, as though his world had been broken and remade within and without. The answer came like an awakening. Everything in the Sanctuary shone with the same light, but the light was reversed. The relics illumined the Sanctuary; the table shone as though basking in their brilliance. He could not see his own face but felt as though it shone in the blaze of that splendour. Even the lanterns seemed to receive their fire like planets reflecting the sun.

And within himself, that sour, bitter struggle of light and dark was seen for what it was. Not the smug victory of his true self finding God yet hating Him, but the creative enlightening of his soul – whatever that was – by a searing splendour in which his desire to lay blame for the deaths of David and Davina at God's door seemed pitiful in that brilliance. But the splendour was purchased at a price. Somewhere deep inside himself, an enclosing darkness pressed more heavily with malicious intent, like black wings, refusing change.

\* \* \*

Outside the monastery gates the quiet sound of stone against stone betrayed the tread of a boot. The gatekeeper tensed out of a half doze. Late travellers in these times were rare and one had to be on guard; a benighted traveller should not be turned away, but death also kept night hours in wandering bands of men who had set themselves outside the law, and the monastery was undermanned. A fist knocked at the door.

'I'm coming! Who travels so late? We are shut up for the night; I can direct you on but cannot admit you.'

'Robert! It is I, Hérault! I travelled all day: let me in.'

'Hérault? Why so late? Could you not have stayed somewhere until dawn? You know the rule.'

Grumbling, Robert fumbled with the bolts. 'The Prior will hear of this... Rules are made to be kept... He will not be pleased...' The postern swung back. Hérault had stepped back a few paces and Robert moved into the doorway to hasten him in. Beyond, over Hérault's shoulder, the gatekeeper saw a sudden movement as the cross-bolt caught him in the throat.

\* \* \*

Stephen almost gasped under the pressure of the enclosing darkness. He felt trapped between dark and light. The radiance of the relics enthralled him just as long as he kept his mind on them, but if for a moment he turned his eyes to the surrounding blackness it seemed to be sucking him in while the force of the light seemed to drive him away. In those periods he felt his old hatred return. Why could this be allowed? Why this confusion of desire, this struggle of light and dark, of life and death? If this force was in the relics why did it have no power over darkness? Darkness had no power – darkness was mere nothing, the absence of light.

\* \* \*

In the courtyard Hérault swiftly entered through the postern gate, followed by two dark figures who flanked him as he crossed the open space. They reached the dormitory doors which Hérault tried and found open. He did not enter but sent one of his men back to the postern. Presently three more entered and crossed to the dormitory – they all carried long knives. After the briefest of pauses, four went in.

Hérault and his lone companion stood awhile outside but no sound betrayed what was taking place within. After a while Hérault moved away alone towards the Prior's quarters.

\* \* \*

The blackness pressed in, intensifying and enervating, until Stephen felt he was about to pass out. He felt simultaneously that he was dissolving into a vacuity of darkness, driven into it by the force of the light from the reliquary. He tried to return to his prayer: he was, after all, a Keeper. He might mistrust or despise the relics but he could keep his vow. There was perhaps a handhold on sanity here, a chance to say, 'I detest you, but you will not see me weaken for that. I have a vow of vigilance over you, and if you are weak I will be strong. You cannot defeat the darkness but you will not drive me into it.'

He focused on the cloth. It was worn and not altogether clean. It was dusty, but not with the accumulated dust of time; indeed, the whole Sanctuary was remarkably dust free. To his knowledge, no one had the job of cleaning it – strange that he should only just have considered that. Someone should be caring for it. If these things mean so much that a continuous prayer vigil is held over them, why is no one charged with the simple office of cleaning? Looking around, he was puzzled even more by the evident fact that it was unnecessary. Do the relics have their own invisible servants? Do they serve themselves?

He suddenly realised that he no longer felt the fearful oppression of surrounding darkness. The towel shone with such a brilliance that in spite of his terrors a few moments ago he felt as though power was passing from it to him. It seemed to be speaking to him, not in words but in emotion.

'Here, see! Touch and feel! I am here for you. Be clean!'

Stephen raised himself to his feet and moved forward but stopped again. He was a Keeper; it was for him to serve, not to be served – and besides, hadn't he vowed privately to himself to serve his vigil to this rag in spite of it, not because of it? He pulled himself up to his full height and turned back to his station.

He looked into blackness.

A black void screamed away from him into infinity. Before him was nothing but shadow, and the pressure of light on his back drove him forward.

\* \* \*

Blood spread from Brother Phillip's habit where he lay face down on the floor. Hérault cleaned his knife on his back. He was disappointed, not that he had killed him – he would have done that anyway – but that he had got so little from him beforehand. Phillip was the Prior's right-hand man; he had looked up in surprise as Hérault entered his cell and puzzled at the abrupt question: 'Where is Stephen?'

'Stephen? Why? Hérault, you have no business with him. He is in seclusion keeping the vigil. Why are you returned so soon?' In two strides Hérault had Phillip by the throat. The force of the attack carried Phillip backwards to the wall, striking his head and pinning him there.

'Where is he?' Phillip was too stunned to reply. Hérault pulled him forward, forced him to his feet and dashed him back again against the wall. He pressed his dagger through Phillip's habit, pointing upward below his breastbone hard enough to break the skin.

'You are dead if you do not answer. Where is the vigil held?'

'The vigil is sacred, Hérault. You are in peril of your soul.'

'Stephen is a Keeper. What does he keep?'

Phillip drew in his breath but the cry was crushed in his throat by Hérault's strong grip. He kicked out and the dagger pressed hard in response.

'One last chance, Phillip. Answer me and you live. Where is the vigil held?'

'On your soul, do not ask.' Again he drew breath for a shout only to have it choked in his throat once more. Hérault thrust deep. 'I abandoned my soul years ago to a richer cause.'

As Phillip died, the two men stared into each other's eyes, Phillip's filled with pity and dismay. Hérault's remained empty, vacuous of all feeling. Not until Phillip died did Hérault release his grip on his throat, withdraw the knife from his heart and let his body drop to the floor.

\* \* \*

Blackness closed in and opened out before Stephen in the same moment. All sense of time other than that of infinite, unending time was lost, as was all sense of place other than infinite blackness. Was this hell, eternity? Terror and fear and loss screamed from his whole being. There was nothing to cling to, only this formless horror. Where was he? Who was he? Without form and void he had no sense of identity. His name? His name was Stephen. He must cling to that. His name was who he was. His name was his identity; if he could hold on to his name he could survive this. This – what was this? He was lost in a black nothing, the blackness of death, or something worse than death.

Nothingness poured from his eyes into a non-universe devoid of stars. Stephen – he was Stephen, but he could not find himself. Nothing but black emptiness – falling in all directions at once from nothing, into nothing. All there was was all he could be – nothing.

The relics, where were they? What had become of his vigil? The relics had been real but he was infinitely distant now. His vigil had been a service to them but they had driven him away. And yet they had wanted to serve him; how could they have pushed him into this ghastly void? He was there to serve them anyway, not to be served. He had turned away from them – yes, he had turned away. They had not stopped him. Why not? Not because they were mere pottery and linen. He had been forced to accept that they were more than that. They did not – could not? – destroy the darkness or prevent him turning away because, whatever they were, their nature was to serve. He was worth nothing unless they served him. If only he could find them now he would not turn away again; his one act of service would be to let them serve him. He was nothing without them, and how could nothing serve reality?

He searched the darkness for a distant spot of light and began again the vigil prayer. A smothering sense of futility almost made him stop, but he pressed on. After all, what else was there to do? Futility alternated with resentment. They had let him down – or perhaps he had let them down – but he had not understood. He did now and was sorry. He wanted to make amends. Why would they not let him? Petty retaliation? Spite? He would not behave like that; why should they? He could give in to the darkness. He could do it now; it would be death of a sort, but it would be their fault, not his. It would be a release. Just give in… their fault, not his… do it now, why not?

He did not. A battle was going on. He felt he was fighting against an unknown adversary – against the light or the dark? He could not tell. Then it was as though they were fighting over him, and finally he found he was fighting himself. Somewhere inside him a spark of his real self was fighting the dark, nihilistic monster he was in danger of becoming.

* * *

The Prior moved slowly to his feet from prayer. He did not look at Hérault or the group of men behind him. Instead he turned to his lectionary and began to read aloud.

* * *

Stephen saw, as in a dream, the towel and the broken jar. They still shone, but with a light no longer their own. There was no table. Two figures – one standing, one kneeling – regarded him steadily. The kneeling figure, a woman, appeared to have been crying. She held the broken jar which glistened with oil from which came the heady scent of balm. It filled Stephen's lungs and permeated every part of him with a strange combination of soothing and longing and grief. Some of her hair had caught on the broken edge of the jar. Her hair was dusty and moist, but the moisture was of her tears, not balm.

The standing figure was a man who carried the towel tied around his waist like an apron. Some trick of light made the dust appear to outweigh the towel. Not outweigh, perhaps, but somehow to exceed it, and yet the towel, for all its apparent age, seemed quite unworn. The dust it bore was the dust of ages, from a cleansing of the world through all times.

'Help me!' cried Stephen. 'Clean me! The darkness is destroying me!'

'Do you know me?'

'You washed your disciples' feet.'

'Love is a two-way exchange. If you cannot receive, you cannot give. For them their cleansing was their need to serve in proportion to the power they were about to be given. They needed to be cleansed of their pride.'

'And I?'

'Oh Stephen, yes you are proud, but you are far, far from being like them. For them their pride was their main soiling. Once that was cleansed the rest fell away, although not at once. For you it is a far deeper thing.'

'My sin?'

Those eyes which can see far deeper into a man than any other pierced his soul with pain, but the pain was not his own.

'Stephen, I washed away your sin long, long ago.'

Stephen could not speak. He knelt.

'Stephen, you need to be cleansed of your hate.'

'I hate myself.'

'That is not possible, though many have thought so. You hate me.'

'No! How can you say that?!' He began to rise to his feet and turn away in the same movement, but checked himself, horror-struck.

\* \* \*

The Prior turned the pages of the heavy Bible and found another place. The men watched in silence, uncertain, their eyes switching nervously from the Prior to their leader. They had been promised riches and power beyond imagining. They had killed a dozen or so futile monks and searched the main buildings, the chapel and the outhouses and found nothing. Now they watched while this old fool read Latin from a book, but they did at least know what the book was.

Hérault stabbed his dagger down through the pages. The Prior began reading as though nothing had happened.

'Your monks are dead; your monastery is dead. It seems we have been a little over zealous.'

The reading continued, quietly, unfaltering.

'You have, shut up within these walls, enough riches to clear this land of poverty or to rule it forever.'

Still the monk continued.

'Since you hoard riches or power – or both – and provide for no one, old man, perhaps now is the time to consider how you might use it for yourself, with our help.'

The reading concluded with the words, in Latin: 'He said this not out of concern for the poor, but because he was a thief and stole for himself out of the common purse.'

The Prior looked up. Hérault withdrew the dagger.

\* \* \*

The towel and the jar were on the Sanctuary table as though nothing had happened. Stephen had been about to turn away as he had before, but this time stopped short before it was too late. The thought of returning into that void froze him in the action. His eyes had fixed on the towel, seeking an anchor against the dark. The man and the woman were gone. The dust glittered disconcertingly on it with the mysterious quality of a shifting mist or a sea fret in which uncertain images competed for his attention. He knelt and reached forward, taking the towel's lower, free-hanging edge and raised it to his eyes. The dust danced and sparkled before him, difficult to pin down. Voices rang in his ears; a deep humming rose and fell with a palpable physical resonance. One particle on the cloth loomed on his vision, so large he felt he should have been aware of it from the beginning. He withdrew his head a little but the particle loomed larger, as though it was approaching him. Blurred reflections danced in its depths. The fragment sparked and flashed, bright light against shadow, growing every moment until it filled his vision. Reflections blurred into shapes and shadows. Sounds jarred in his ears like a half-heard conversation on the edge of consciousness.

He blinked at the blurred outlines as a scene slowly emerged. A group of men, half a dozen or so, were arguing in a room. One in particular, a thickset bear of a man, shouted profanities at another. With a shock Stephen recognised Hérault who stood quietly before the onslaught with a strange smile on his face. Stephen heard a semi-coherent litany of threats and demands. The men in the room apparently expected booty or payment from Hérault and he had not delivered. Hands were on weapons. Hérault had a knife in his hand but it was held unthreateningly down. With a start Stephen saw it was wet with blood. He became aware of a bundle of clothes on the floor behind Hérault and almost simultaneously saw it was a body. A cry of horror escaped him – the Prior! He could see no wound, but the awful stillness and the bloodstained dagger presented an unmistakeable message.

'Patience!' Hérault was saying, addressing the angry man. 'Would you throw everything away just as it comes within your grasp?'

One of the six moved behind him but it was a move that could have been alliance rather than insurrection, and Hérault ignored it as though he had not noticed.

'I bought you with payment in advance and the balance is to come. Is this how you would repay me?'

The man before him raised his knife threateningly, but Hérault shrugged and made to turn away. The other seized the moment and raised his dagger for a strike. Stephen could scarcely follow what happened next. Hérault checked his turn and spun back, squatting slightly in a move as balanced as a cat. His arms spread, raised a little above shoulder height like a skater maintaining his balance. Nothing else seemed to have happened, but the big man rocked slightly and looked surprised. He opened his mouth as though puzzled and blood gushed out. Still with a look of surprise he appeared to hiccup and his throat welled red. His right hand wavered, clutching his knife as though he did not know what to do with it, and slowly he collapsed forward onto the floor. Hérault stepped sideways as he fell and appeared disgusted at being splashed with the spray from the man's throat.

'We still have work to do and the way is clear. If any more of you wish to drop out just let me know.'

The man who had somewhat ambiguously fallen in behind him now stepped forward to his side. 'We'll strip this room bare, then the chapel.' He turned to Hérault: 'We are with you. Oxenden was a blundering fool. I would have finished him myself soon!'

'Very well! We have to find the entrance to the Sanctuary. It is unlikely to be here but it must be searched.'

Hérault and his second-in-command moved towards a door beyond the lectionary. The man took the opportunity to murmur in his ear, 'They still cannot be trusted.'

'We can attend to that later.' Hérault turned. 'You, Olaf!' he indicated one of the men, 'Come with us. You two, search everything in this room. Strip the panelling if you have to. If you find anything we will be in the chapel searching more thoroughly this time.'

'If they find anything they'll keep it to themselves.'

'Is that what you would do, Bertrand?'

'I've got more sense. We need each other, you and I.'

'Just keep a watch on this one; we'll deal with the others later.' Hérault strode down a corridor towards the chapel. 'Somewhere in this monastery is a treasure guarded by one man, a Keeper. I know him. I rehearsed him, played him like a fish and made him mine. He was one of five Keepers – now the only one – who kept vigil in turn. I could have made him lead us to the Sanctuary.'

'Why didn't you?'

'Because I did not know it would be his vigil. It should not have been, but now the last man alive who knows the whereabouts of the Sanctuary, and the only one who would have led me to it, is shut up in the Sanctuary itself.

'No problem. We hold the monastery – we can just wait. Sooner or later he must come out.'

'He cannot come out!'

'He will have to!'

'He cannot come out. The Sanctuary is sealed from without by a heavy stone that is rolled into place and unreachable from within. Each Keeper releases the previous one who closes the stone behind him, sealing the tomb as he leaves.'

'Stupid system!'

They entered the chapel by its main doors. Two candles lit the altar and the lamp of the presence burned above it. The altar candles stood high on two sandstone pillars, one on either side.

'He'll suffocate!'

'What's that?' Hérault stopped almost in mid-stride.

'He'll suffocate, shut up there like that. We'll never find him!'

'Of course, you are right! He should but he does not. Why do they not suffocate? There are burning lamps in the Sanctuary – he has told me. There should not be enough air for him to survive, or the lamps to flame for long.' Hérault paused. 'There must be an air inlet. Search for holes in the wall or floor.'

\* \* \*

With an effort, Stephen closed his eyes to the horrors he had seen and threw himself on the floor in distress. After a few moments he looked up. The Sanctuary table was above him. The arms of the towel extended down to him as though in compassion. He raised himself to his feet and returned to his post. The lanterns flamed as ever and the relics and table shone as before. He dare not look away again, but he could look at the walls across the table. Seen in this way they were not irredeemably black. They glistened like jet. Facets in the walls gleamed like stars. Why had he not seen this before? He looked at the wall to his right, but except for a torch flaming in its bracket the wall was black and featureless. He became aware again of that consuming, uncomprehending darkness. Hastily he looked back across the table where again the wall sparkled with stars. Some trick of refraction made the wall only visible when seen with the table in view.

How had he seen and heard Hérault? The man was evil. It was impossible that he would have helped him. He must hate everything the monastery stands for. What had he said? 'The last man alive who knows the whereabouts of the Sanctuary...' The last alive? Why should he say that? Were the other Keepers dead? Had Hérault killed them? He appeared to have killed the Prior, and Stephen had seen him kill one of his own men. How could he possibly have helped a man so filled with hate and avarice?

Hate – he had been told that he was soiled by hate. Were he and Hérault brothers in hate? His vision swam with tears, running the reflections in the walls, the candles and the relics into an incomprehensible confusion of light and shadow. Blackness mingled with fire, shapes swam again before him in which once more Hérault moved, he and his men searching the chapel for the Sanctuary. Try as he would he could not shut out the vision. He knew now that he and the Sanctuary were intrinsically bound up with Hérault's search and the deaths in the monastery. An unwilling observer, he watched as the scene unfolded before him.

# 15

## August 2008

Hérault released his hold on Scanlon's shoulder. Scanlon rose to his feet and looked around him. Hérault's discord had faded to a mere backdrop of sound in which the monastery ruins stood in detailed clarity with that pervading sense of loss which had nothing to do with the erosion of time. He looked steadily around, getting his bearings. He knew he was outside the chapel but there was no evidence of it now. Away to his right he could see the cistern by which he had slept that first night after his escape. His eyes fell on the gatepost beside it. On the other side a mound in the turf betrayed the presence of a second post fallen to the ground. Where was he looking? He half closed his eyes and took his bearings from the remembered chapel. Surely the trough was inside it? Mentally he stood up the second post, one each side of the heavy lidded trough like two pillars flanking a table. An altar. Of course! It was the old altar table dressed with a cloth of moss. He rebuilt the chapel doorway in his mind. It had been no more than four feet from where he was standing with a mediaeval Hérault framed in it. The Hérault now standing with him was the same man – surely he should know the monastery layout?

Scanlon looked around again. Very little of the old walls remained; virtually nothing on which to get a bearing. Without his immediately recent vision of the working buildings he could not possibly know where he was. Hérault continued to harangue him. Peremptorily Scanlon held up his hand to stop the distraction and, remarkably, for a short time Hérault did stop. Scanlon looked intently at the twenty-first century scene. He looked, felt, listened and tried to surrender all his senses to the name-sound, expecting conflict between it and the discord, but found none. The discord was there behind everything. He knew he had only to surrender to it to bring back the ancient walls and courtyard. He felt the harsh summons even though Hérault remained silent. It reached out to him and touched him. Deep inside he felt it touch the pain within him that was becoming just a numb memory. It touched the disease and wrenched pain from it; just a second of pain that tensed his spine and brought sweat to his brow, and in the pain was a threat and a command. 'Death or survival, Scanlon? The choice is still yours.'

Hérault spoke with a quiet menace. In spite of the sudden pain Scanlon tried to open himself to the name-sound. He felt sure it would fight back against this evil menace. The deep harmonic palpated through everything. But it did not fight back.

He could physically feel it, but to his dismay it did not counter the discord but seemed to complement it. If the discord was a backdrop, the name-sound was a foundation – no, not a foundation; a structure. It permeated everything as the fabric of a canvas permeates a painting. Far from confronting the threat it somehow offered meaning to it, and the discord, although threatening to Scanlon, did not react, any more than darkness reacts against light. Looking to his left Scanlon saw the ruined walls of what must have been rooms beyond the chapel. They shimmered slightly as in a heat haze. The call of the Namestone became deeper, producing again that bodily sense of resonance that had felt like a command, only now it was more like a hand held out to him. Calling rather than commanding, it carried an echo of Hérault's words.

'Death or Life, Frank, the choice is yours.'

Suddenly and briefly he saw the monastery complete again, but this time with no sense of loss. Every detail was there as before, but the awful clarity conjured by the discord was gone. Not because he saw less but because he saw more, as though a brilliant picture had suddenly been replaced by the real thing. He felt the flagstones beneath his feet and a warm flow of air from the chapel door. The mediaeval Hérault still looked out towards him. The vision faded as quickly as it had come, but in that instant he saw a widening of that Hérault's eyes and a start of awareness.

\* \* \*

Hérault leapt forward through the chapel door into the cloister, his knife before him, but was momentarily blinded by the transition from the light into darkness. Motionless, he listened intently as his vision returned. He had seen a face peering at him from the shadows but now cursed his precipitate reaction. There was no sound of movement; the cloister seemed deserted and yet the face he had seen in the light of the chapel doorway had been clearly defined. It was not Stephen's, so who could it be? Some monk who had escaped the killing? He knew all the monks; it had been none of them. One of the men he had left searching the Prior's quarters? He felt not, but was less sure.

Slowly, keeping to the wall, he moved to his right. Because he carried the threat of these hired men in his mind he was inclined to believe it was one of them. There was substance in this. He knew that without positive results he could not keep them under his command much longer. Killing that fool Oxenden had brought them into line for the time being, but it would not last. Perhaps they were already forming against him. The Prior's quarters were on the other side of the chapel but one of them could have come around another way. If so he would be making his way back with little to report. No, the threat was there but action would not come yet. He had deliberately divided them by taking the main threat, the powerful Olaf, with himself and Bertrand. Perhaps the time had come to deal with Olaf now. He would do it himself or give the task to Bertrand – either way it would leave the remaining two easy to slay. Bertrand was right, and as he himself had known all along, they had been needed for the killing but could not be trusted for the search. They would conceal whatever they found, and they would attempt to snatch anything found by himself and Bertrand. With the prize in their eyes they would be a far more lethal alliance than they presented at the moment. Divided they were ready for slaughter. Bertrand himself would be a tougher nut, but that could be left until later. Hérault had no illusions. He was single minded and calculating. At the end of this he was going to be the only one to carry away tales or spoils. He made his way back to the chapel.

He could not have been more wrong. The face in the cloister had been no spying scout. No negative report had been taken back, and insurrection was under way.

\* \* \*

Back in the twenty-first-century daylight, Frank turned and again confronted Hérault with new eyes. Everything trembled in a new perspective, a sort of double vision. Harmony and discord, understanding and knowledge – no, not understanding; something both less and greater than that, and immeasurably greater than mere knowledge. He felt rather than understood the difference between life and survival, and with it he looked into his cancerous pain. Hérault had not taken it away, after all: he had masked it and was now using it, twisting it like a knife within him. Survival was being offered, certainly, but at what price?

'Death or Life', and in that name-sound call he knew that mere survival was death. He sought his pain in the name-sound and found it. No healing, no anaesthesia, but a wholeness that made the cancer irrelevant; no longer something to be fought or denied but simply accepted because there was more important work at hand.

'Leave me! Get away from me!'

He lashed out at Hérault's face with the back of his hand and Hérault staggered back. Scanlon was surprised at how weak the man was. Behind him he saw again the demon shape in cloud or smoke, threatening and dark. Did it sustain and cajole Hérault as much as Hérault had been trying to do to him? Was it some demon controlling Hérault? Or a demonisation of Hérault himself? It was almost recognisable but only at the edge of vision. If he looked directly at it, it vanished into the shapes of clouds and treetops.

Hérault raised his arm, and at once the cloud-demon became more visible, as though he had summoned it. Scanlon felt an oppressive presence, the tight grip of pain in his chest. He saw again that dark threatening shape and heard the discordant command driving him back, building the mediaeval abbey on its twentieth-century ruins. He saw the dreadful clarity and raised his hand to shut it out. Desperate, he sought the name-sound and at once was conscious of its greater harmony upon which even the discord depended as shadow needs light. Strength returned. He saw the cloud pouring down like a whirlpool into Hérault's upstretched hand but felt only anger. In the presence of the name-sound this discordant power was a blasphemy. Without further thought he threw himself forward, seized Hérault's hand in his left and struck him in the face with a forceful back-handed sweep of his right. He put more force than he knew he possessed into that blow and was astonished to see Hérault crash backwards to the ground and lie still. Frank recalled his surprise at the deterioration he had observed in Hérault when he had returned to the monastery with Tim earlier that day. Whatever power Hérault was drawing on was draining him physically.

He looked up the slope beyond the ruins to the debris where he had first hidden from Hérault and his henchmen, and where just a few minutes ago Anselm had stood and Tim had been shot. He felt again that sense of centrality, of everything being relative to another reality. It emanated from that pile of rubble. He moved towards it, oblivious of Hérault who lay behind him. As he went, the name-sound washed over and through him, calling, growing. He passed beyond the chapel and the further ruins and once again the ancient monastery walls grew around him, strong this time, complete and shrouded in night. He was alone.

\* \* \*

Alone in the benighted cloister, Hérault approached the chapel door. A sudden noise from within stopped him outside the doorway. Hefting his knife once or twice in his hand he stepped quickly through, glancing left and right. At the far end of the chapel by the altar screen Bertrand faced Olaf and the other two hired men, his dagger drawn. Hérault approached noiselessly up the centre aisle as the three spread out, Olaf to Bertrand's right and the other two circling to his left. Suddenly Olaf made a lunge at Bertrand who sidestepped neatly and slashed at the man's arm. In his turn the man leaped back and to the side, parrying with his own weapon and attempting to seize Bertrand's arm with his free hand. Hérault was still about thirty feet away. He shouted a peremptory command and the group froze for an instant. Setting his eyes on Olaf, he slowed his pace to a casual stroll.

'What? Squabbling like children just when we have our prize?'

The leader scowled, his dagger still turned on Bertrand.

Two paces closer.

Hérault kept his voice level and calm. 'I suppose if we kill each other the booty will be fair game for the first scoundrel to enter the place.'

The men stood before him in a parody of a stage setting. Another pace; four more and he would be within striking distance. Four, five; Olaf's dagger half turned towards him. Six… Bertrand misjudged the moment.

Spinning away from his assailant he thrust his dagger into the breast of the nearer of the two men circling to his left. The man's jerkin was leather, a tough protection against a dagger thrust, but the bodkin was honed razor sharp and Bertrand was strong. It burst through the jerkin and pierced between the fifth and sixth ribs, driving upwards into his heart. In the same instant the man struck hard with his own weapon but, lacking both Bertrand's power and patient hours of honing, the blade was turned aside. Olaf, however, had space and time to swing his arm like an axe. The combination of the trunk-like arm and the massive blade sliced into Bertrand's spine. Hérault was still a pace away. Bertrand crumpled like a rag doll even before the man he had stabbed to the heart had begun to slow down.

The man's fellow, seeing Bertrand fall, assumed they were now three to one against Hérault and turned, emboldened. Hérault had not faltered but his main quarry, in turning his attack back to Bertrand, had maintained their separation. Seeing Hérault's concentration on Olaf, and assuming the loss of Bertrand had given him pause, the second man launched his attack, reckoning without Hérault's alertness and speed. Scarcely taking his eyes from the big man before him, Hérault ducked down and to the side. The blow passed high and Hérault swayed and struck upwards into the man's armpit, severing the brachial artery, his blade passing through vessels, tendons and bone, trapping in the shoulder joint. He twisted the knife to widen the space for withdrawal but Olaf, towering over them, brought both his fists down on his colleague's shoulder blade and arm, pushing heavily down onto Hérault's upthrusting hand. Seizing the agonised man's arm he used it as a club, crushing it into Hérault's face. Twisting the man's upper body in a powerful grip he hurled him to one side, wrenching

Hérault's dagger from his grasp. Hérault found himself weaponless under a towering enemy.

He was saved by the man Bertrand had stabbed. His heart shuddering in a death spasm, he fell between them. From his crouched position Hérault launched himself upright and backwards. The other stepped to the side of the bodies on the floor, expecting Hérault to make for the door, but to his surprise Hérault made use of the separation to slip by him up the aisle towards the altar. For his size, however, the man had fast reactions and a good turn of speed. He followed on the run so they arrived at the altar only a few paces apart. Hérault threw himself across the table, one hand clasping the silver crucifix and the other clutching at the altar cloth. He half turned and cried out, 'Sanctuary!'

His attacker stopped, astonished, for no more than a moment, then with a sneer launched his dagger thrust. The moment's pause was enough. Hérault continued his turn, bringing cloth and crucifix with him, scattering the altar candles in a torrent of molten wax. The cloth passed between him and the blade, deflecting its aim. He smashed the crucifix into Olaf's face, the corner of the heavy base rupturing his right eye. Kicking at the man's groin he became entangled in the cloth, falling back against the altar. Nevertheless, his first blow had brought his assailant to his knees. He raised the crucifix again and brought it down on the man's head. Behind him one candle still leaned almost upright, its flame spreading up the worn, gold-threaded tapestry of Christ and Mary in the garden.

With an almost spasmodic movement Olaf lashed out with his dagger deep into Hérault's stomach. Hérault brought the crucifix down again onto the man's wrist, driving it deeper in but breaking his hold. Again he struck Olaf in the face with the crucifix, then dropping it, seized the dagger, plucked it from his own stomach and in the same movement slashed it across Olaf's throat. Flinging up his arms, Olaf straightened his legs in a sudden rigor. Rising to his full height with his arms stretched above him, he swayed there, blood gushing from mouth and throat, his fingers searching for a hold. They found a slender silver chain. For a second longer he stood, then like a falling tower he collapsed onto Hérault, bringing down with him the lamp of the presence in a shower of burning oil.

Hérault screamed in rage and pain, trapped beneath the man's body as the altar cloth ignited around him. Seconds later, in a rain of molten gold thread, the burning tapestry fell over them like a shroud.

All this Stephen watched in the dust of the towel.

*'Sancta Maria, Mater Dei, ora pro nobis peccatoribus, nunc et in hora mortis nostrae...'*

The flames took hold in the chapel, spreading in the roof beams and the tinder-dry hangings.

*'Deus, refugium nostrum et virtus, populum ad te clamantem propitius respice...'*

With no one to fight it, the fire quickly gained and grew, drawing air in through the chapel doors, then as the leaded glass buckled and blew, it burst out through the gaping window eyes. No one prevented its spread to the neighbouring buildings; no alarm sounded in the dormitory where the sleepers lay in a slumber from which neither fire nor fury would rouse them. The blaze grew until the roof timbers gave way and the fierce outpouring at the windows was momentarily sucked in and then burst out again with renewed ferocity.

*'Sante Michael Archangele, defende nos in proelio; contra nequitiam et insidias diaboli esto praesidium. Imperet illi Deus, supplices deprecamur: tuque, Princeps militiae caelestis, Satanam aliosque spiritus malignos, qui ad perditionem animarum pervagantur in mundo, divina virtute in infernum detrude.'*

In the Sanctuary, Stephen said Mass before the reliquary table for the souls of the Prior and the monks in a broken, gasping voice. The Sanctuary air remained clear and fresh but above him hungry flames sucked the air and filled the monastery with choking smoke. Timbers fell in showers of sparks and burning ash. Neighbouring trees blackened, leaf edges curled and smouldered red, and a black shroud of smoke, shot through with ghastly hues, rose like a demonic wing into the night sky.

*'Misereatur tui omnipotens Deus, et dimissis peccatis tuis, perducat te ad vitam aeternam...'*

He no longer looked into the towel. The images there were too distressing, and the deaths of Hérault and his men afforded no satisfaction. Rather they enhanced the horror and futility of it all. And so he did not see the cloud in the night sky take shape, nor did he remark on the strange billowing that gave it the appearance of some diabolical creature dancing over the inferno. Had he done so, he may have been struck by the unnatural contortions in its whirling mass that made it appear to descend for a moment back into the heart of the flames as though it would enter again into the chapel to claim its rightful prize, taking to itself in the way faces are seen in the fire, the tortured features of Hérault.

A moment later it was gone.

Stephen did not feel trapped. Somehow the relics, particularly the towel, conveyed security and freedom. Nevertheless, he felt doubly bound to the Sanctuary by a desire to serve and be served by the relics, or those they represented. Aware that he alone of the Keepers was left to preserve the vigil, he resolved to continue as long as his strength lasted. He needed and prayed for absolution, and said Mass for the souls of the murdered monks. In the absence of the Host, and with no priest for consecration anyway, he could only recite the forms and liturgy.

Time, much time, passed. The air stayed fresh and the lamps continued to burn. The Sanctuary was continually new as though time made no mark there. Stephen felt himself in the presence of the eternal. In the presence, but not part of it. He felt the passage of time acutely in his emotions and his increasing weariness. He marked off the time by reciting the hours by guesswork: Lauds, Prime, Terce, Sexte, Nonnes, Vespers. Once he tried again to look into the dust of the towel, hoping to see the outside world and perhaps someone still alive, but was granted no vision apart from the dust itself, heavy as the weight of the world's sin.

*'Dies irae, dies illa, solvet saeculum in favilla...'*

Verses flowed through his mind and lips in a confusion of grief and fears. Bitter regrets, self-blame and horror mingled with prayers for the souls of the dead, but he finished no prayers; he wandered in the litany and the hours. Deep inside him a hard, tight knot refused to unravel. He averted his mind from it as though looking away from some appalling scene. One by one he repeated the names of the dead – Phillip, Simon, Barnabas... but one name he held back. It was down there in that knot, enclosed in another named Iscariot.

Eventually, above him, the flames that had spread from the burning chapel in wind-fanned showers from every falling timber had nothing more to feed on. The forest, cut back a bowshot on each side, remained largely untouched. The monastery was its own funeral pyre, its timbered roofs and floors producing such heat that stone walls cracked and fell. The lesser wooden buildings, stores and barns had blazed fiercely and loud, but there was no one to hear. It was seen, however. The fury was not spent quickly. Sucking in air with a force that stirred the remote woodland trees, it hurled it to the skies in a pillar of cloud by day and fire by night. Eventually men came to investigate, but when they arrived all was a thick ash bed, too hot to approach. None considered for a moment that deep within that Gehenna fire one still lived. Even had they done so, they could have done nothing.

The heat did not penetrate the Sanctuary. If fire is purifying, no purification reached Stephen. Deep inside him was a knot of ice, many-layered and hard. The air around him remained as did the Sanctuary itself – pure and apart. It did not feed the flames nor suffer their fumes. The Sanctuary was complete in itself; sustaining, not sustained; containing, not contained.

Stephen looked up. A woman was standing between him and the reliquary table. Tenderly she looked down at him, her eyes brimming with compassion. She stretched out her hand. He rose and went to her. She led him to the table, took up the pitcher and passed it to him, indicating its broken neck as he took it. He looked into its depths. The interior was dark. The black hairs that clung to its broken rim seemed to be an extension of its night-sky blackness. Each glistened in the light of the lamps and drew darkness from the interior. There was an unexpected sparkle to them. He peered more closely. Like the towel, fine grains of dust clung to them. His eyes widened. Dust from the feet of Christ. He looked round into the eyes of the Magdalene and saw in their dark pupils a mirror of the world.

Mary continued to gaze at Stephen as though patiently waiting for him to fulfil some task. The heady perfume of spikenard emanating from the jar gave a dreamlike quality to his thoughts. Was he looking into her eyes or the jar? Did tears or balm glisten at the rim? He felt warmly enclosed, sustained by enfolding arms just as the arms of the towel enclosed the pitcher; arms heavy with the dust of all worlds.

*'Dust thou art...'*

Mary stood, her arms held out a little towards him, not enclosing but encouraging. His sense of oneness with the pitcher grew – oneness with the pitcher, the dust on it and on the towel; the dust of the feet of Christ, of the apostles, Mary's hair, her tears and the balm; Mary herself, all bathed in the Sanctuary light and sustained in those greater enfolding arms.

From some distant place, so distant that it was within him, he saw the Oneness of all things. Hopes, desires, dust and dreams, all sustained and sustaining; the vast and terrible darkness in the Sanctuary walls, the hot smouldering fires above, sustained alike in the Oneness. All were one in the vigil, and the vigil was eternal, 'even unto the end of the world...'

How had he ever thought the vigil had been his? Or any of the Keepers'? There was one Vigil and one Keeper in whom all things had their being, and without which, nothing... nothing.

Deep in the woodland below the ruined monastery, leaves rustle above the shaded facets of a flowing brook which lazes its way among the outcrops and tree roots. Occasionally it fills the air with a tinkling sound like that of a child playing on the high keys of a harpsichord, and descends by greater or lesser degrees, often silent and invisible, shrouded among tussocks and undergrowth, until splash by splash it grows, fed by the watery ooze of marshes and occasional rivulets which join their sister to become a running stream. Sparkling downwards through the steep woodland, it widens here, narrows there, dropping musically for a few inches then spreading over an outcrop to soak silently down a broad mossy face. Soon it can contain these silences no longer. Every downward drop becomes a rush, dashing spears of light from the rocks wherever the sun breaks through, and at night filling the moist air with the steady sigh of its progress.

Day follows night. Mosses and ferns arch over the stream and carpet the woodland floor. Leaves drift from the canopy overhead, singly and in windswept clusters. Clusters grow to swirls and swirls to a steady fall. Not all enrich the loam beneath – they hang spiked on briars and drift into tree hollows, and some flutter lightly into the brook to be borne downstream until caught on exposed tree roots or trapped on the stream's stony bed. Few make the journey as far as the pool in the woods, and fewer beyond.

# 17

He was tired and weak with the passing time. Mary still stood there but he knew that time for her was as time in *God*, a day as a thousand years and a thousand years as a day. She shared in the eternal Vigil. Once again he felt himself in the presence but not part of that particular newness of the Sanctuary. Above him he knew rather than felt that the ashes were cold, a cold stained without and within. Deep inside him that multilayered knot of hate was as cold as the ash and as hard as ice. Stephen continued to turn his mind from it. It had no place here but he felt powerless to cast it out. He was conscious of the weight of ash above as though it pressed directly on and into him, compressing the hatred, hardening it, bearing it down into his mind, pressing it into himself. Vainly he tried to ignore it, to keep his mind on the vigil, the Sanctuary, Mary, but he could not overcome the pressure of the ash. He tried to call out but it overcame him as though his hate was drawing it down, adding its own pull to that dead weight.

He looked into Mary's eyes and was caught again by the depths in her pupils. Tears glistened in them like stars. Her eyes filled his own vision and he felt himself drawn into them as though plunging into the sea. He saw himself there. Not just a reflection but as she saw him – lost, distressed, shamed, filled with a pity and a compassion that had no outlet and which vied with hatred for survival. He saw clearly for the first time two sides of himself, totally incompatible and mutually destructive. He tried even more to look away from that ice-cold knot and see just his duty and his distress for the destruction and killing he had witnessed, but they seemed too weak and pitiful, perilously poised on the brink of some black pit into which they could pour to be lost forever. What value was compassion when it was so fragile? What value duty, when hatred could render it sterile?

'Look deeper, Stephen. Unless you overcome yourself, you will destroy yourself.'

The words were Mary's but the voices were many. He fancied he heard the Prior distinctly, and Phillip and many others, not as a chorus but each one distinct, alive and personal – even the voices of David and Davina, and yet there was a sense of each being a harmony in Mary's voice, and hers one of something greater.

'I cannot!'

'What do you fear?'

'My hatred of Hérault eats into me. It sets my blood on fire!'

'You do not hate Hérault.'

'I detest him! He was a foul murderer! I would delight in his death except that it prevents me from killing him.'

'Look deeper, Stephen. Your hate is not for him.'

'He was a traitor! How could I have been taken in by him?!'

'Were you?'

'Of course! I… you know…' he faltered.

'Look deep, Stephen.'

Deep in Mary's eyes that image of himself was all too real. A torment of conflict between two doomed facets of himself; a hazy sense of the man he could be who wept with grief for the destruction and death, and another who trembled on the brink of a black pit of loathing and self-destruction.

'Help me!'

'I cannot, and He who can, can only do so if you will make the journey with Him.'

Stephen felt himself not so much torn apart as on the verge of a catastrophic implosion, a complete collapse into annihilation. How could he go into that abyss and survive? In the fathomless black of her pupils he saw the ice-cold pit within himself, as dark as that endless space into which he had been hurled at the start of his vigil. Then the monastery was there to return to, even if he had not known it. He was poised between hell without and hell within.

'Help me! Anything! Where else can I go?'

He looked into the abyss and all the compassion, all the pity, all he felt to be of any value in him, poured into that pit, consumed in a torrent of hate. He felt its destruction into drab tatters like rags in a fire. He felt the despair of futile hatred, for Hérault who was dead anyway, for the treachery which had destroyed so much and for the futility that it had all been for nothing and based in error. His vision clouded in a furious mist of rage and futility. He was powerless; the events that consumed him were past and gone; he could do nothing about them and yet they could still destroy him.

Where was *God* in all this? A red tide thundered in his blood. *God*! If *God* was in this at all it was without love. What father would treat his children, or let them be treated, like this? An inarticulate cry escaped him, unframed in word or thought, but somewhere in his emotions between expletive and prayer.

Everything that he felt that was of any value in him had turned to dross in a hot tide of rage which was sucked to annihilation in the ice-cold core of hate within him, as ice cold as the rage which bore him down was hot. He felt himself falling with it, and over, in and through all the choking ash blanking out everything, cutting him off from all hope. Where was he? Where was *God*?

'Help me! I have done what You asked! Where are You?'

The change was as sudden as it was unexpected. He was no longer alone. Something he did not understand infused him.

'What do you see?'

He found himself staring into his own heart, sinews and blood. A vast cosmos, a universe contracted to his human frame, hung before him for an instant, and in that instant vanished. Just the core remained, a poisonous heart, numb cold, towards which he fell but came no closer. Time and space combined in a frame that kept him forever falling, forever watching, sustained with a strength not his own.

'Look!'

He felt himself reaching out like a child to some deadly plaything, but at the same time being guided like a child whose hand is held by a skilled teacher in performing a new and difficult task. Two layers of reality, and a third, that it was not his hand that would perform this dread task but the Teacher's. And a fourth more dreadful, that it was his will that had to command. That he and the Teacher were in some way one, mutually empowered and imperilled. To fail was annihilation, and to do nothing was to fail.

He was plunging from a great height towards the blackened, ash-strewn remains of the monastery. Swirls of ash coiled in the wind, too far away for him to feel heat if there was any, but it was cold and lifeless, a fire long burned out and abandoned. Shadows and scorch marks scarred its surface. Other shadows flicked among the ash-swirls with the grotesque appearance of life in death; of movement in a death mask, a cold, dead nightmare parody of life: cracked stones, charcoaled timbers and cold swirls of ash grew menacingly as he fell. The sense of a death mask intensified.

The malice that had destroyed the monastery, the monks and the other Keepers was locked there in an ice-crust of greed. It bore the features of Hérault and a terrible seductive rationality; a deep permafrost destroying from within; hard, and intensely powerful.

'I can't destroy this – I cannot do it! That hatred echoes my own. It is far too strong for me!'

'Stephen, to destroy it would be hard for you but not impossible. Your task is much harder than that. You must pass through it.'

'Through it?'

Again the sense of vertigo gripped him. He had passed some barrier and was plunging from an impossible height into an ice-world of his hatred of Hérault and Hérault's hatred of him. Shards and splinters of greed and loathing split and cracked into Hérault's terrible grin. He fell ever closer; soon he would be close enough to strike. There would be just one chance at the moment of contact to lash out and shatter the ice teeth and the grey permafrost eyes; to destroy and be destroyed; hate exterminating hate, just seconds away.

'Pass through!'

'Do nothing? I cannot!'

'Vengeance is Mine – not yours! Pass through!'

Stephen uttered one cry of loss and despair and, plunging into that frozen morass, surrendered himself entirely to the mercy of *God*, and did nothing.

Nothing.

The horror was gone as though it had been a sham, a non-thing capable of harming him only while he feared it. What would have happened if he had tried to destroy it?

CB

Leaf by leaf, layer by layer, the forest floor grows. Autumn winds scatter the canopy, down to the tree roots, out across the moorland, and in swirls across the monastery ruins.

Few visit the monastery site. Ground ivy and brambles grow over the path and thin, scrubby bushes take hold among the fallen stones. Martins nest in the upper and lower cliffs and wild rabbits make tentative scrapes in the ash.

Leaping from rock to rock, rushing through gullies, dancing in the sunshine and defying the shadows, the stream pours into the pothole above the pool, echoes from ledge and boulder, boils in the blackness and passes through rock fissures back into daylight, and just occasionally a yellowed autumn leaf rises with it to the sun.

CB

# 18

Still he fell. Beneath him now, but much farther away, another landscape – so far away that he lost all sense of falling. A wide land, perhaps the whole country, mist-shrouded and dark, spread almost to the limits of his vision, so dark and hazed that he had difficulty in discerning a landscape at all. Cloud obscured very little. Only the wracks rushing by him impinged on his vision. Was it a landscape? The land, if it was land, was bounded by uniform grey. Sea? Beyond that speckles and freckles of more land, and farther still a darker grey, and around that a dark abyss like night sky, seen fleetingly in the moment it expanded out of his vision as he fell. He felt as though he was plummeting towards the whole world and for a moment wondered what had happened to the Sanctuary, and in the same moment saw it both from within and without. From without, from his great but falling height, it shone as a bright spot in the surface of the earth, like a bright eye looking at him from a mirror. From within, it was like looking into his own heart, a bright chamber, red and pulsating in the flickering light of the Sanctuary lamps.

He saw it not from his votive position before the reliquary table but from above. The table was there, and the artefacts. The lamps burned as brightly; all shone in a gleam of flame, bright as stars in a desert night. He saw himself prostrate before the relics – still, unmoving, unnaturally still. His vision reddened the colour of blood. Anger at his failure, his duplicity and the ease with which Hérault had expected to use him surged uselessly against the hard reality of the body below him. A body, nothing more, except that it was his own lifeless corpse. Was even that taken from him? Not life – he could cope with loss of life, rejoice in it even, but how can one extract blame from a corpse? Blame? Yes, blame; his hate needed an outlet.

He recoiled from the Sanctuary and saw again the world from above, much closer now. He fancied he saw his own face staring back as one sees features in a distant landscape, a face in the moon. He viewed his own hate in that face, pitiful and loathsome, all his despair, the feeling of being deserted, deprived, unloved and therefore unlovely. Folly, weakness, fear and futility: all that he hated in himself, and all that he was.

'You made me like this! I am not all to blame! You gave and You took away and You brought me to this!'

'I brought you to this, Stephen. This is a gateway you must pass through.'

'I don't understand. If I am so hateful, why not destroy me? Is this some horrible game? Am I being used for Your sport?'

He threw himself in rage and pain at the landscape below him. How could this be? What had he done? Everything was lost: Hérault, the monastery, the Keepers' vigil, the Prior and the monks. And Hérault had led him on, and he had been so willingly led. Had Hérault only continued because he had found so tainted and willing an accomplice? Anger and hatred boiled again and choked in his heart and eyes. He fell deeper into the abyss in an exploding confusion of futile fury with no focus except the cold destiny below him.

'Damn it!' Damn himself, damn the world and the Sanctuary. No, perhaps not the Sanctuary, but himself? Had he really died? Had he seen himself dead? Was there nothing left but this boiling, pointless hate? A stream of self destruction bore him down to the earth, hard and detested below him.

'Pass through!'

'No!'

He threw himself into a last frenzy of death. Why listen? Why not die now? Not the mere bodily death he had seen in the Sanctuary but now, a true death, the second death, absolute and final, why not? Now!

'Pass through!'

He was saved by simple curiosity. What if he did not die now? A spark, an infinitesimal link to that voice which held him back from destruction, or rather sped him through it and beyond, kept him from the finality he so ardently desired.

He did not die; he passed, and in the Sanctuary, that which had been his body and bone, which he had thought of once as his main, his only, hold on life, began to crumble to dust – one with the dust of the towel.

Time, much time, passed.

With time there was regrowth in the scorched earth where the monastery had stood: mosses and ferns, sparse grasses, insects on waving stems and dewponds, blown leaves from the autumn woods, all nourished by sunlight and rains, living, dying, forming a new fertile layer, clothing old death in new life. Centuries of new life and regrowth. Boys came from the villages below, exploring, roaming and swimming in the pool.

St Anselm's was used as a storehouse, then disused, lived in again for a short while, then disused again. In later years it was used intermittently as a camping barn.

# 19

The sky, fierce with stars, spread infinitely before him. The great wheel of night and day turned above him.

Πατερ μου      ο εν τοισ ουρανοισ...
*Father of us all*    *who art in the heavens…*

He did not know then what fires blazed in the heavens or how they burned, but he did know that they blazed to the glory of *God*. That same hatred that had lost both Hérault and himself as its focus could not be quenched in the icy reaches of space. It turned once more upon *God* himself. Echoes of old angers clashed within him, but where did self end and else begin? What boundary lay between himself and *God*? What powers were his and what *God*'s? Surely if all power was *God*'s, then what of this fury, the destructive furnace that he carried with him? Was this crucible capable of destroying its own Maker? The sense of having no bounds pervaded him with power as though he and the heavens were one. Here was the power to destroy the absolute. He listened for the voice which had brought him this far.

Silence.

'Where are You?'

Silence.

'Will You not speak to me now? Do You know that I have the power to destroy You or release You?'

'You have no power against me except that which I have given you.'

'And that I must and shall use, but show Yourself.'

The stars were suddenly extinguished. A single light burned bright and steady. Stephen saw a man, small and far away, with his arms held out to him. He paused, puzzled, on the brink of recognition, and as he looked the man filled his vision, not as though he had drawn closer but as though there was nothing else to be seen. His arms, although held out willingly and invitingly, appeared constrained. All over his body wounds dripped blood – his hands and feet, his head, his side and, Stephen knew, from his back as well. Behind him, although he was free of it, stood a gallows cross, itself pierced and blood-stained like a parody of the man.

Here in the vast heavens was a focus of the infinite made finite. A centrality that gave order and place to the whole as a hearth gives to a room. The rage boiling in him found its chaotic fire directed at this affront of strength reduced to weakness. His emotions became a tidal race poured into a single channel. Everything he had ever felt or hoped or cursed was sucked into that final rush, and somewhere in the depths, like a leaf trapped on the bed of a fast river, something began to lift and stir, drawn against its will into the flood.

Drawn as to a vortex, he felt rather than saw that the light, the cross and the figure of Christ were aspects of one another, shown to him like the images or visions in the dust of the towel. They carried that same sense of complete reality. More than that, they bore all reality in themselves. The stars had not been extinguished; they were there in the light and the cross and the man. He saw the whole creation from without in three forms that were somehow one; not the Trinity, but a trinity nonetheless.

'I did not ask for this!'

'You asked Me to show Myself.'

'I did not ask Christ to die for me!'

'I do not die for you; I live for you. My life is your life.'

He was seized again by the torrents that consumed and possessed him. Death was very near, oblivion within his grasp. He had become a maelstrom of the elements of his being; his hatred both a lava flow and a glacier, his destruction a tornado and a landslide, all pouring into a vortex of oblivion that would take even the light of creation with it into darkness, nothingness and non-being.

And in this, a leaf, frail and light, lifted and turned in the turbulence; a fragment, a particle of his soul, carried without its will. A tiny, weak, despised part of him that wanted to live and to love.

'… and to be loved!' A still, small, woman's voice spoke quietly and tenderly: '*God* is good; His love endures forever.'

Nothing more, although that tissue of his soul strained to discern it. Just the voice of the Magdalene, harlot turned saint who, when the world was moved to murder, anointed his living body for burial, washed it with her tears and dried it with her hair. The greater part of him ignored it, sweeping all to oblivion in its rush. Growing with his anger, his power hurled itself upon the defenceless Christ and the cross, and most of all upon the compassion they displayed. He had not asked for compassion. He despised mercy. Every petty distress, every major loss, bereavements, pains, the wasted hours and years, cried out for annihilation not mercy. What did *God* know of mercy? Where had He been when Stephen had cried out in agony and loss? Why had he been so easily duped by Hérault? Why had Hérault been allowed to survive to work such evil? And all for nothing – nothing!

Nothingness, oblivion, was the end and the answer to it all. On this cross he could re-crucify *God* and himself together, or destroy himself and the cross and *God* with it. Had he not seen all creation, the stars and lamps of the heavens there in the light that illumined both cross and Christ? All of himself, his hated self, there. His past, his future, Hérault's past and future, too. Here he could at last vent his hate and his despair and destroy both together. And *God* – the author and sustainer of this misery? He could destroy him, too, with all of his creation, and if he failed, he at least would not survive to know it.

The vortex grew black. Everything poured into it, even the light of creation. Hate, filth, despair and loss: nothing could escape that pit. The cross distorted into a warped grotesque of itself, and the scourged and crucified Christ opened his arms to the flood of fire, ice, rock and storm and was consumed.

One tattered remnant, drawn into that pit as it fell, clung to the cross like a wet leaf in the wind. 'Lord, remember me when you come into your kingdom!'

Small, despised, weak: one fragment of Stephen's dying soul clung to life in the unmaking of the heavens and the earth.

'Pass through!'

'No! No! I cannot! I cannot!'

'If I die, you must die with Me. Come, pass through.'

'What have I done?'

'You have made death, and I die with you. Pass through into My death; it is not as yours. Your death is mere oblivion; Mine is to be crucified upon all creation. Pass through into My death.'

The cross filled his vision, so close or wracked that it was no longer recognisable. And yet, as before, he saw from afar and near at once. Every part was filled with a burning intensity.

'I am too weak. I cannot—' Stephen tried to thrust the vision away. 'This is too hard for me.' The very words seemed futile.

'What is weakness? You have destroyed all creation. What is left is all there is – all there is is you. You and I and the cross are one – behold! See what you are!'

All creation burned in the cross like a sky full of stars.

'Who are you?'

Who was asking the question and who was being asked?

The cross burned with a fierce, flaming light. It hung in the darkness like an intense gemstone, a stone with a heart of fire.

'Who am I?'

'What do you see?'

'A stone, as bright as the light of creation.'

'This is your Namestone. It is all creation. Your name is the unquenchable light with which it burns.'

'How can I be this? Must I be forever alone?'

'A harp string can sing with many harmonies at once, but it is one string, and ultimately one song. Your name – your light, is just one of many harmonies. Reach out and take your name.'

He reached out and touched the fire which was his name in the harmony which was within that name above all names. He felt again the bounds of a human body, a hand with which to grasp, and pain in that searing, purifying light which flowed through him and gave him being. In that instant he saw all the suns and stars of space to its utmost bounds and knew them for what they were; saw all the harmonies that were not his and yet were; saw the course of creation in which they all sang the eternal anthem, past and future. In that great antiphony he understood the past and much of what was to come.

* * *

The pain at last subsided. The light became a lesser light, held in his hand. The Namestone was shielded from his sight in the pouch on the girdle of his restored monk's habit. The confusion of light and shadow coalesced into the well-known landmarks of the upward climb to the now long-dead monastery to which he knew he must return. His feet trod the familiar path upward in the darkness, guided by the lantern in his hand.

Somewhere ahead a faint voice called. He struggled with the woodland path. The voice called again. 'Hello! Is anyone there? I'm lost!'

# 20

Scanlon, shutting out the discordance of Hérault and whatever demons controlled or were controlled by him, followed the call of the Namestone. He found himself alone in the monastery, in a dark corridor. He struggled to see in the dim light to his right and left. A strange light from the night sky filtered in from small roof-vents above. A similar glow appeared to come from a window along the corridor to his right. He knew the chapel must be that way and had no desire to go there. In any case, the call of the Namestone came strongly from his left in the direction of the faint window light. He went that way, half conscious of a smell in the air.

The corridor opened through an archway into a room from which there were two doors out, and a window at the far end. There were tables and chairs laid out almost like a schoolroom with a very few books on the shelves. Perhaps it was a scriptorium where monks would have sat patiently and carefully illuminating manuscripts and scrolls. It was really too dark to see clearly. Scanlon went to the window, the source of an orange glow that swelled and faded irregularly with an underlying flicker of fire. Looking out he saw smoke billowing high and to his right with the occasional swirl of sparks. Something was burning fiercely some distance away out of his line of sight.

He became aware of the smell of burning but could see no flames, just firelight reflected in the smoke. He looked around nervously and was startled by a deep crashing sound that was difficult to locate. The room grew brighter and, turning back to the window, he saw the drifting smoke reflecting a much brighter glow. Running to the archway by which he had entered, he was met by a hot wind from the corridor, at the far end of which he made out a faint glow. There was very little smoke where he was but the heat seemed to be increasing. He wondered for the first time where everybody was. He had no doubt that he was actually in the monastery and not just seeing it. The strangeness of this no longer overawed him; too many strange things had happened in the past few days, and somehow his ability to be here centuries ago helped to make sense of Anselm and Hérault appearing in the twenty-first century. He half made to enter the corridor, but the hot wind carried a sense of menace.

Hérault! He had seen him in the chapel which must be at the end of this passage. It must be the seat of the fire. Some sense of duty made him venture a step or two into the passage, but the heat was getting intense. Besides, Hérault must have survived for him to have come into the twenty-first century. The glow at the far end brightened and began to flicker with flames. A sudden instinct made him turn and run.

As he re-entered the scriptorium he heard a loud eruption behind him. He turned towards a door in the opposite wall and almost threw himself at it. Somewhere near it he struck a stool or low table and half fell, struggling to maintain his balance in a ludicrous pirouette. He fell backwards against the door, scrabbling at the latch behind him. Diagonally across the room the archway to the passage erupted like a blowtorch; books and papers on the shelves opposite burst instantly into flames and a huge fireball filled the room. He would have screamed but an opposite reflex clamped his mouth and eyes shut.

The door was not fully on the latch but it was heavy. His weight, perhaps aided by the pressure of the hot air, bore it back behind him and he rolled himself around its opening edge in a wave of blistering heat. The advancing fire saved him. He was blown aside by the sheer force of the hot wind into the shelter of the still opening door. He threw his weight against it but could scarcely resist the pressure. Gasping and sobbing, he tried vainly to close it.

The scriptorium window blew outwards under the pressure, showering its fragments into the valley below. Sections of its roof lifted, and the roof of the chapel corridor gave way completely. Scanlon, pushing at the heavy scriptorium door, suddenly found it as light as a feather. It closed with almost no effort, drawn by the suck-back on the other side. He grabbed frantically at the ring handle, but the latch engaged on its own. For the moment he was safe. A pain in his legs made him look down. His trousers were smouldering in bright patterns like soot on a chimney flue and he beat at them frantically. He was gasping for each breath.

There seemed to be no air and the heat was intense. Surprisingly, there was still very little smoke, which he assumed was due to the intensity of the fire beyond the door. Running his fingers through his hair he found it crisp and singed. God! How his face stung! The cry *God!* hung in the hot air. It rang in his mind like a growing echo; a prayer or a curse? But it faded rapidly as he looked around.

He was in another passage into which the same fearsome light entered through covered roof-vents. He could see swirls of smoke caught in the light, pouring up and out, and wondered where it came from. He was still leaning against the heavy scriptorium door and felt it hot at his back. He was sure it would be burning on its inner side and knew he had to get away, but still he stood, trying to catch his breath. It was like trying to breathe in a vacuum. He peered up into the rafters, his eyes still a little dazzled from the flames. Smoke coiled through the beams above him towards the vents, with tiny pinpricks of light floating lazily with it like drifting fireflies.

As he watched, one of the fireflies grew into a bright cluster which broke into a burst of tiny sparks. He spotted another cluster which grew similarly but remained static, not drifting with the smoke. As it grew it lit up its surroundings. Strands of cobwebbed straw hung down, twisted and charred in the heat.

Birds' nests! Years of old nesting material filled every cranny above his head! Much of it must have ignited in the first flash but had extinguished in the subsequent vacuum. Strands still glowed at their tips but could not reignite in that atmosphere, but a few seconds' change of wind and the whole roof void would be ablaze. Scanlon forced himself to move. Pushing himself from the door he half ran, half stumbled down the passageway. There were doors to rooms on his right which he ignored, first because they were too close to the advancing fire and then because he reasoned they must open into rooms backing on to the cliff top and offer no means of escape.

Every few paces he glanced up at the roof vents but the smoke still poured steadily outwards, much lower now as though it could not escape fast enough and was slowly filling the corridor. He reached the end before he found a door to the left opposite another to his right. The corridor ended in what appeared to be a cupboard. The smoke was now at head level and he had to stoop to breathe. The left-hand door had a solid handle and no visible latch. Scanlon pulled at it but it resisted. He pulled harder, then pushed. It was either locked or jammed. He struggled frantically with it for precious seconds, then turned in panic to the other door which had a thumb latch. It opened easily and he was startled to find that the room beyond was brightly lit. For a moment he feared the fire had reached it by another route, until he saw a lamp in a bracket on the opposite wall.

Before entering he reached for the cupboard door in case it had a window or other access to outside, but as he did so he heard and felt a sudden thump in the air. Rolls and billows of flame poured through the roof void and once again he found himself leaping through a doorway to an uncertain refuge. He slammed the door shut, his heart pounding with the exertion, pain and lack of air. He closed the latch and looked around. To his astonishment he was not alone. A woman was standing, watching him from the far end of the room.

He gasped, 'Is there another way out of here?'

She remained quietly watchful, not moving.

'I'm sorry! You don't know who I am, but the monastery is on fire!'

A woman was the last person he expected to find there. She was small in stature, dressed in clothes that were not out of keeping with her surroundings – a plain brown habit with a lighter headpiece. The effect was soft and gentle, and somehow knowing, as though she was fully aware of the effect she created but at the same time could do nothing about it, and had from the plain certainty of her religious demeanour, committed it wholly to God. Scanlon felt abashed at his own appearance, both as a man before a beautiful woman and as a man who, having been the unwilling butt of circumstance, is confronted by someone so self-possessed that it seems nothing untoward could touch her at all. Nothing untoward to her, that is. She looked on him with compassion as though she saw all the suffering and weakness of the world in him, strongly, almost fiercely, but completely in her own possession of her own soul.

How could someone possess anything so completely that they had equally and evidently given wholly to *God*? To offer her help would have been grossly naive. It did not occur to him. He was the one in need.

'Help me!'

'O Frank, can you not see, feel and hear your own destiny? If you can, then you can take it yourself.'

He was taken aback by her use of his name; not so much by her knowing it – his recent experiences and the depths of understanding in her eyes made that unsurprising – but that she should use it. It was a name that he had always considered to be mundane and uninspiring. From her lips it seemed to hold meaning beyond anything he had imagined. Christened

Francis, he had been called Frank before he had any choice in the matter, and it had proved too hard to change again.

'Frank is older than Francis,' she said, echoing his thoughts. 'Francis is simply a Frankish man, one who was so named for being frank. You know it to mean honest, but before that it meant free, and before that it was a lance thrown free to do what it will in battle. By your name you know yourself, and others know you as you know them by their names. Scanlon means a quarreller, but names in this world are partial. Your true name comes from *God*. In the uniqueness of your own name-song you will find your completeness in the One Song.

'Here you are running away from more than fire. You must go back; only there can you achieve your destiny. You must find its expression in free action in your own times. It was not for nothing that you were so named.'

'What is my destiny?'

'Go back, Frank. Your destiny is written in your name and your name in your destiny. Can you not hear its call?'

Suddenly the call of the Namestone thundered in his blood. It sang high notes in his pain, so that the fear, exhaustion and pain were no more than the threshold to something far greater that called to him from beyond the very earth on which they stood.

Behind her he saw a large round stone, like a millstone in a grooved channel, partly hidden by lesser stones so that a casual or even a determined observer might not recognise its purpose. Indeed, had Anselm not described it to him that first day he would not have known it himself.

'This is the Sanctuary?' he asked, gesturing towards the stone. It was more a statement than a question.

'You must enter it in your own times, Frank. You must go back.'

'The name-sound called me here.'

'The name-sound carries the echoes of all times and all places. It is the song of the stones of the children of *God*. You hear it because you are a child of *God*.'

'And Hérault, what of that sound?'

'He also is a child of *God*, no less than you. He allied himself to another, also of *God* but fallen deep and far away, whose sound is also a part of the name-sound but twisted into disharmony. Listen for the true sound that calls to you alone. It is an echo of your own true name.'

'My true name? Do I have a Namestone?'

'Each child of *God* has a Namestone. It is the child's true name which lives in the Name above all names, in which we are all made one. Before your name can be complete, you have much to overcome. Then your stone can be given into your own keeping.'

'What are the Namestones? Surely they are more than stones?'

'They are dust, like all stones, as you yourself are dust. They are the focus of *God*'s love, just as you are.'

'I do not feel His love focused on me.'

She laughed. 'Not one speck of dust exists without His love. It encompasses all creation and the smallest mote holds it all. You are many motes, Frank.'

'And the Namestones? How is His love divided among them?'

'His love is not divided; it is all, and in all. All creation is one, and the harmonies of the song of creation, which is the song of the stones, is one song, the song of the Word made flesh.'

'Or made stone,' said Scanlon bitterly.

'Ah, Frank, you have much to learn and much to overcome in yourself. What you see as stone is not what we see, and what you see as flesh is not what we see. Once I saw my own flesh as you see yours and sold it for bread. Then both my flesh and my heart were stone as you would see stone, but I knew it no more than you know now.'

'This is far too difficult for me. How can I be one with all creation and not lose myself?'

'What you see as yourself, living and moving and having your being, is no more than an image in a glass, a focus. It is the image of the harmony that is you taking its part in the song of creation. Your Namestone is your other focus, the image of the song of creation holding you in itself.'

'But if creation contains all the songs, all the harmonies…'

'Ultimately all the stones are one Stone, all the songs one Song, and all the loves one Love. Not one of the harmonies is lost except it wills it.'

'This is b… this is stupid! I can only half understand what you are saying. What do you mean by "except it wills it"? Does anyone *will* to be lost from creation?'

'Frank, you must go back. These things must be learned in your own song and your own time, not here. Time here is short. The monastery has not long before it is consumed in the fire.'

The name-sound grew in his ears, mingled with the roar of flaming timbers and cracking stone. A crash sounded behind him. Turning, he saw the door split down its centre and tongues of flame reach through. The roof above was smoking as that in the passage had been.

He turned back and found himself alone. Where had she gone? Who was she? He looked at the stone in the channel. It had not been moved. There was a small unglazed window in the wall on which the lantern flamed, but it was far too small to be a way out. He moved towards the Sanctuary entrance stone and placed his hand upon it. The name-sound grew with the same sense of compulsion he had felt when he lay beside the pouch at St Anselm's. He crouched, still with his hand on the entrance stone, as the burning door cracked and buckled behind him. Just a moderate pull should set it rolling back, exposing the entrance behind it, but still he waited, mesmerised by the name-sound.

He closed his eyes and concentrated on the call of the Namestone. Could he trust it? If it failed him he would die within the next few minutes unless he could escape through the Sanctuary. Where had the woman gone? He had a firm grip on the entrance stone, and the crackling of the door became a roar as the fire broke through. Once again the temperature soared to burning point and the flames fed on the air in the room. And again he was by a door, this time of stone. His lungs could take little more. There were blisters on his hands, and his nostrils flinched at the stench of his burnt hair. The roof timbers twisted and shrieked in a high-pitched whine above him, modulated by the deeper groanings and rush of fire.

If he were to take this escape route, what purpose would it serve? He would die sooner or later anyway. Nevertheless, fear was a strong master. He gripped the stone and pulled, but the pain in his blistered hands weakened his grip and his fingers slipped. The fire shrieked in a discordant fury, sharpening his fear. Sobbing with the effort he grabbed at the stone again, gasping at the hot, depleted air to prepare for another try. The fire roared loud and hot in his ears, driving and commanding like the discordant clamour that had emanated from the demonic familiar from which Hérault had drawn power. *'Another ... fallen deep and far away,'* the woman had said. It was driving him into the Sanctuary. His hands pulled again at the stone and he felt it shift. One good heave and the way would be open; open for him and the fire to pour through.

He hesitated. Why did it feel like rape? He was being driven to find safety, and every opening had brought him closer to the Sanctuary, hounded by the force of the fire. And what was within? A bare chamber containing ancient relics which were probably false or forgeries. He would not be able to move the stone back from the inside so the little air within would be sucked out to fuel the fire even if the fire did not enter. Perhaps there was a Keeper at vigil within? If he entered they would probably die together. If he did not, the Keeper would die anyway,

These thoughts rushed through his mind as the fury lashed at him, and in all, under all and through all, the song of the Namestone called him to follow – follow where? He did not know.

'Go back, Frank!'

Gasping, with his eyes shut tight, he fell across the stone and gave in to the name-sound. He heard the roof explode above him, a crashing roar, pain and a brightness that shone through his clenched eyelids, and then silence.

## 21

He lay a long while, smarting and burned. His nostrils were full of acrid smoke but he could still breathe. He took long, desperate gasps of air. The light through his closed lids was painful to his eyes. He opened them a crack but the pain was too great, and he closed them at once. Fresh air filled his lungs and presently he began to revive. Cautiously he tried to open his eyes again and found himself adapting. His hands still clasped the entrance stone and it was the first thing he saw clearly. It seemed changed: not the smoke-blackened disc he expected, but old, weather-beaten and mossy. The channel it ran in was clearly visible, as was the fact that the stone had been moved to expose a trapdoor-sized opening. Had he pulled it back? Even though he was getting used to it, the light still hurt his eyes, preventing him from seeing clearly. It was daylight but the terrors he had passed through still pressed too close for him to understand what was happening.

It took several minutes before he became aware that he was lying out in the open daylight of the twenty-first century on the rubble mound where he had hidden from Hérault and his men several days before. He was farther back than he had been before and could see the hole into which he had half fallen before attempting his escape down to the woods. It was now enlarged by the movement of the entrance stone, and the rubble sloped steeply down into the entrance. To his surprise he saw a slither of footprints going down into the opening, and patches of what appeared to be blood.

Tim! Or could it be Hérault? Someone with an injury had entered the Sanctuary. Frank peered into the entrance but could see little. Stone steps descended in a spiral to his right. He heard nothing. If Hérault was down there, however weak, his powers were formidable and he still had the gun. After some hesitation Frank entered cautiously, taking care not to dislodge the loose slope of stones. He began to descend the steps as quietly as he could and after just a few turns saw light below him. A few steps more brought him out into a lamplit room. He immediately recognised the Sanctuary from Anselm's description. Tim was sitting on the floor below one of the flaming lamps, deathly pale. Anselm stood by him, and the reliquary table, just as Anselm had described it, was on the far side of the Sanctuary, some distance from a wall of black stone. Frank found the distance hard to judge. There was no sign of Hérault.

'Tim!' Frank was at his side in a couple of seconds. 'Thank God! I thought you might be dead! I should never have got you into this!'

Tim looked at him through half-focused eyes and made to speak but the effort was too great. Frank looked round at Anselm. 'Can't we do something? He must be bleeding internally!'

'All that can be done will be done.'

'Will he live?'

'All *God*'s creatures will live, but whether he will live in your time is in your hands, Frank.'

'What must I do?'

They both turned at a sudden clatter of stones. Hérault appeared at the foot of the stairs, gun in hand. For a long moment everything came to a stop. Frank was again struck by Hérault's physical deterioration. Surely it was less than an hour since he had struck him to the ground and escaped into that sixteenth-century inferno. He had left him unconscious and possibly injured, but Hérault appeared before him now as a wreck of a man. Whatever power gave him his extraordinary abilities appeared to be draining him physically. He had slipped down the last few steps, scarcely able to stand. His eyes were hollows and his cheekbones stood out as though they might burst through the sallow, paper-thin skin. Only the gun gave him any sense of power. He stared feverishly about him, at the lamps, the walls and the relics, at Anselm and Frank, then back to the relics, barely glancing at Tim. His hand holding the gun trembled intermittently, making Frank more nervous of an accidental than a deliberate shooting. Finally he looked long and hard at Anselm.

'So, my friend, we prove difficult to kill, you and I.' He leant back against the central stair pillar. 'Here we are, where we could have been centuries ago without all this.' He gestured with the gun towards Tim to illustrate the word *this*. Anselm did not reply. Hérault pushed himself away from the pillar and moved towards the reliquary table with a perceptible jerkiness in his movements, as though he had to consciously control every action. Anselm remained quiet but moved with him to the table. Frank was torn between a desperate desire to help Tim and a dread of sparking off another shooting. Suddenly overwhelmed by the pain of his burns and his complete sense of helplessness, he collapsed to the floor at his friend's side.

'Hang on!' Tim's voice came out as a whisper and he moved his hand onto Frank's arm. Frank turned and leaned over to him. 'Do you still have the stone, Tim?'

Tim nodded and opened his hand. The Namestone lay in his palm just as it had lain in Anselm's several days before. The reflections of the lamps glittered and swirled in its flecked surface as the firelight had done in St Anselm's. Frank knew now that those bright flecks were more than mere reflections. There was a strange quiet. The name-sound, the call of the stone which had led him through the burning monastery and finally into the Sanctuary in the twenty-first century, seemed to be held in abeyance; not a mere silence but a sense of completion and waiting. Frank looked across to Anselm and back at the stone. The woman had said that in some way he did not understand, Anselm and the stone were one, or aspects of one another.

Frank took the stone from Tim's outstretched palm. 'Why didn't you give it back to him?'

Tim shrugged. He had little strength for speaking. 'No time.' He clipped the words between breaths. 'He got me in here just before you arrived.'

His whole time in the burning monastery then, and the fight with Hérault beforehand, had occupied no longer here than it had taken for Anselm to get Tim up the slope and into the Sanctuary.

Frank looked at the stone in his hand. It felt light, without the inertia he had felt before. There was an indefinable sense of completeness, of presence rather than centrality. If he could imagine feelings in a stone he would have said it felt good to be there. The walls of the Sanctuary shared many of its qualities: their black reflectivity held a sense of depth rather than enclosure, with the lamplight shining not onto but rather into the surface. He could almost feel that they were shining out of it. Perhaps that was why he found distances hard to judge. And time? Where had the time gone between Tim being shot and his own entry into the Sanctuary?

At the table Hérault gestured animatedly at the towel and the jar. Frank had been so absorbed in the stone that he had taken in nothing of what he had been saying, but he was conscious that Anselm was not replying.

Frank pulled himself to his feet and crossed to Hérault and Anselm, ignoring the gun with difficulty. Just minutes – or perhaps centuries – before he had entrusted his life to the song of the stone in the face of an apparently certain death, and had survived. Now he felt he must entrust the stone to itself and to Anselm.

He held out the Namestone. Anselm took it and laid it on the reliquary table before the broken jar. Immediately the name-sound filled the Sanctuary, as though it was the Sanctuary sound. Frank saw for the first time the flecks in the dust of the towel, the black of the woman's hairs also flecked with dust on the broken neck of the jar, and the play of light in the black depths of the walls. The name-sound was not just coming from the stone but from the whole Sanctuary, which was one with the stone.

'Anselm, what is this place? What is going on?'

'Listen.'

Frank let the name-sound wash through him and tried to shut out everything else. It hung in the air like the resonance of a great bell, filled with a myriad harmonies and sub-tones: *the song of the Namestones of the children of God*. He heard many voices in its depths, subtle and distinct, and yet each was one with the whole. He heard the voices of friends long dead, of family and loved ones lost long ago, times and places that had meant much to him, and wrongs he had suffered or caused, all seen again and afresh in the name-sound with a deep supporting theme: *Behold, I make all things new.*

He found he had shut his eyes and opened them again, half expecting to see the woman standing there, appearing as easily as she had vanished in the burning monastery, but nothing was changed, just the name-sound binding together jar, towel, Sanctuary and stone. Hérault stared with a sneer at the Namestone.

'So that bauble has some meaning for you, after all? Some talisman, perhaps, to add to the superstitious awe of these fake and pitiful relics? What is really here, Stephen? The power that brought you and me back, schooled in speech and mind, was not stones or pottery! My master wants what is here, and you know what it is – or maybe your friend here can root it out for me.'

'I do not know your master, Hérault, but he has no power here. You have been sent alone.'

'True, here I am my own master, which suits me well. And if there is a power greater than his then I have more to gain than I imagined.'

'There is no power but One, Hérault, and it may only be given, not taken by force.'

'We shall see.' Hérault turned, holding the gun tightly, 'What do you make of this, Scanlon? You vanish into the past only to turn up here. What did you find there that led you here? And how did you find your way in?'

'You damned killer…' Frank choked on the words, unable to continue.

'Killer, yes, but – ah! You mean your friend. Yet I see he lives. My aim is better with a dagger or a bow, but I presume your opinion of killing is like my own – whether or not it suits your purpose, like Fenster and Harpin.'

'Neither was my choice!'

'No? But so convenient for you. Your friend's death is less so, but you have a choice now. I can finish the job and kill him now unless you help me. Even if you play for time I think he will bleed to death soon. You have experienced the power I can call upon: it is his only chance of survival.'

'Anselm,' Frank turned from Hérault, 'you said the stone had healing properties. Tim will die without help.'

'The healing of the stone, like the healing of *God*, is a fearful thing. One is never the same again, in relation neither to *God* nor to oneself, nor to the world.'

'Did the stone save you? I saw you dead.'

'I was not dead. I died to this world centuries ago and live in my new name which is written in the stone. Nevertheless, when I am in the world I still live in it in the old way and can suffer, hunger, thirst and be abused in the old ways. But this is not new. He Whom I serve trod a far harder path before us.'

'He whom *I* serve,' interjected Hérault, 'would disdain to suffer thus. He remains untouchable.'

'Which is why he uses you, no doubt,' said Frank.

'I tire of this!' Hérault pointed the gun at Tim. 'I think that one way or another your friend has little time. Tell me, Scanlon, you saw the monastery as no one has seen it for more than half a thousand years. What do you see here?'

Frank looked desperately around. 'Help him, Anselm. I trusted myself to the song of the Namestone and it saved me from the fire. Tim had no part in this.'

'What fire?' Hérault swung around.

'The monastery burned down – I saw you there, in the chapel! I ran to a room with a woman in it who... who...' he found it difficult to continue. 'She told me to come back but I was afraid. I wanted to escape into here. She cared for me as though she loved me but would not let me in, then somehow I lost her. I was there alone in the flames with nothing to keep me out of here but somehow... somehow...'

'Somehow you were weak!'

'No! That is the last thing it was. I was being driven by the fire or something in the fire to force my way into the Sanctuary. Although she was gone it was as though I was being driven by fear and the need to possess her. Breaking into the Sanctuary was—'

'Like rapine! But you hadn't the guts to go through with it!' Hérault sneered.

'Yes, but it wasn't a question of guts needed to go through with it; I was out of control, driven by desire and fear. It was something else – the name-sound and a desire to overcome and hold on to myself.' He turned to Anselm: 'Who was she?'

'The Magdalene. Mary.'

It was not Anselm who had answered but Tim, faint and at the edge of audibility but seeming to permeate the entire Sanctuary like a whisper in the gallery of St Paul's. 'The jar of precious balm broken to anoint his feet; her own hairs still clinging to its broken neck; and the towel from another

155

washing, tied around the waist of the anointed Christ at Passover, bearing the dust from the apostles' feet.'

Tim's voice grew faint. The last few words were halting and forced. He leaned his head back against the Sanctuary wall lit by the lamp above, alarmingly pale. There was the briefest of pauses.

'Enough!' Hérault seemed stung into precipitate action, 'He is dying anyway!' He held the gun levelled at Tim's head for two long seconds.

Then: 'No point!' He turned the gun away. Striding back to the table he levelled its barrel at the jar and, before anyone could move, squeezed the trigger.

Nothing happened, not even the dull click of the falling hammer or a misfire. 'Why – do – the – lamps – never burn – out?' It was Tim again. Frank went to his side. 'Light is – eternal here. – The – only light of *God*. Cordite – is – irrev – irrelev–' Tim closed his eyes and was quiet. Frank wondered if he was trying to say irreverent or irrelevant and decided it didn't matter. Hérault, in a fury of frustration, raised the gun above his head and brought the butt down like a hammer onto the Namestone. Frank flinched as it flashed with a burst of brilliant light in which for an instant the Sanctuary walls gleamed white and Anselm's habit shone like a cloth of gold. Hérault, in silhouette, appeared black.

Frank, clutching Tim's arm, saw the Sanctuary in double vision: the walls white in the light of the stone and at the same time, like a ghost image, the same walls black and non-reflective. There was none of the black refractivity he had first noticed, no light played uncertainly in their depths; instead, there was a blank horror of all-absorbing dark, as though to touch them would be to lose oneself forever. He tried instead to focus on their whiteness but found that equally disturbing. Not the blank absorption of the dark walls but a multitude of spectral colour; not separated as in a rainbow but present in the white, as though all the hues that combine to make white were all visible at once, dazzling to the eyes. Not separate from the white, they were the light and the light was them, each hue distinct like the harmonies that made up the name-sound. They were moving like a great dance, wheeling and interlacing in wonder and delight to the song of the Namestone.

'Light and dark are not opposites. Light is life and truth, and darkness – mere nothing – is powerless over it.'

The voice was that of Mary, from whom sevenfold darkness had been driven out. Why, Frank wondered, must she always be known by the name of the place in which she plied her trade and, as she put it, sold her body for bread? Surely she also has a white stone in which her true name is written, known only to her and to Him who writes it. Perhaps we could not look on that name.

She stood between Anselm and the table, a little apart from Hérault. Between them the relics shone, sharing in the brilliance of the dance, and before them the stone, not one but two: one bright, alive with the fires of life, infinitely desirable beyond what eyes can see, ears hear or minds conceive; the other was black, unfeatured chaos.

Hérault spoke. 'So the stone was the key, after all! And you, madam,' he made a condescending bow, 'have profited well from it, I see.'

'I have life and love, the patrimony of an honest master and friend who would be as such to you also, Hérault.'

'I despise such patrimony. With this,' he gestured at the white stone, 'I may be independent of even that power that brought me here – above any other.'

'Not above any other, Hérault, but the power it has can only be given to you, not seized.'

'Have I not just shown you what I am capable of?' He reached out to the stone but, as his hand drew near, the air between it and the stone burned with deep-blue fire. Hérault

157

snatched back his hand which showed bright red weals across the fingertips and palm.

'For your life and future happiness, stop, Hérault!'

'I have no past happiness. What do I care for its future!'

Hérault again raised the gun like a hammer and brought it down onto the stone.

What happened next came so quickly that Frank was uncertain just what he had seen, but he was sure the gun never reached its target. There was an intensity which spread like a concussion wave in a ball of light that filled the Sanctuary and was gone. Hérault's arm appeared to bounce back. The chamber rang like a bell, and the gun, along with most of the hand that held it, was gone. The white stone shone unchanged. Hérault gave a loud cry, more of fury than pain, and with his remaining hand seized the black stone. Frank was not sure whether he intended to use it as a weapon or to possess it – probably Hérault did not know himself – but Frank saw his fingers close over it, and in closing there was again that peculiar sense of perspective that had imbued the Sanctuary walls. The dark stone seemed immeasurably far away. Hérault's hand, although clasping around it, seemed to reach far into the distance in seeking its object, as though he grasped from the Sanctuary some distant dark star. The sense of inertia and centrality that had been absent from the stone while it was in the Sanctuary returned in its darkness.

Hérault reached not up to a star, but down to a pit. He still stood in the sanctuary but his hand, arm and shoulder seemed to lengthen and be dragged away from him. His hand was frozen around the distant black stone as gradually and destructively his body was drawn down to it. He began to scream but his mouth distorted and stretched as his neck and head followed his shoulder. His whole body followed and there, far away, where his hand had clutched the stone, it flowed onto the surface like magma until all suddenly vanished together.

Frank, Tim, Anselm and Mary were alone in the Sanctuary.

Outside, a dark shape clung to the upper cliff where the rocks rang to its discordant fury.

## 22

Frank gasped as though he had not taken a breath for several minutes. Mary and Anselm stood at the reliquary table where the relics lay undisturbed, the Namestone painfully bright to the eyes, lying before the broken neck of the jar. Mary stepped forward to where Tim had slid down and was now lying on the floor. She knelt beside him. Frank joined her. Her head was inclined as though in prayer. For a moment Frank feared his friend was dead, but Mary looked up and smiled.

'I am saying thank you to *God* for Anselm, that he has come through this safely, and praying for you and your friend that you may do the same.'

'I don't understand. Aren't we safe now? Tim must not die here. None of this was his doing.'

'Death and life are very close, Frank. Truly this was none of his doing, but he suffers and is near to death. Remember your name, Frank. You must live it.'

A distant sound echoed in the stairwell to an accompanying clatter of stones. Frank clutched at the pain in his chest and side which he had forgotten in the heat of the past hour, but of which the sound from outside came as a bitter reminder.

'Hérault!'

'No. He is gone as dust in the wind. He sought the unattainable, complete power and complete independence. The only absolute independence is non-existence. Existence must always be coexistence. The recognition of this is the beginnings of love.'

Frank looked down at Tim. He felt deeply responsible. Leaping back to his feet he rushed to the stairs and gained the Sanctuary opening, slipping on the stones on the steps and scrabbling at the loose slope. The harsh command that had first conjured the monastery before his eyes filled the ruined slopes;

more of a command than ever, powerful beyond reason and promising beyond hope. Every desire, every loss, every attainment in his life echoed in its dissonance. He came out onto the ruined outcrop, drawn by the sound. He looked about him. There was no difficulty in discerning its source. As long as he looked directly as the sound drew him, there it was: a bat-winged grotesque, clinging into the surface of the overhanging cliff. Only when he looked away did it appear to dissolve into rock-shadows and crags, the very reverse of when he had first seen it behind Hérault, whose fury had weakened its control. Now, without Hérault, the creature's disharmony tore into Frank, feeding on his desires and his fears.

The creature or demon directed swirling darts of power at him, just as Hérault had pulled down a maelstrom of power from it then. Not singly this time, as it was through Hérault's upraised hand, but a complex and purposeful onslaught, wreathed in cloud. His arms were pinioned, his blood fired, he felt again the sensation of a thousand skittering insects and the anaesthetising of his pain. His arms raised without his volition, his parasitic cancer began to subside within him, not this time with the sense that it was being anaesthetised, but destroyed cell by cell, tumour by tumour. Frank found himself striding across the ruinous slopes, arms held out to whatever demon was summoning him, suddenly devoid of pain.

'See what power I have! See what I can give you!' The sulphurous eyes regarded him from the crag. Without the creature making any apparent effort he felt himself propelled to the downward edge. 'I can throw you down and smash you to oblivion, or –' he was seized and flung out over the drop in a vertiginous scream of panic, 'or I can let you live unharmed.'

His feet crashed painfully onto secure rock again. The voice sneered, 'Lest you strike your foot upon a stone!'

Frank sank shivering to the ground. 'Hear me, Scanlon! Power, Scanlon! Power to survive; power to destroy; power for anything you desire!'

Colours, shapes, patterns flooded through his brain. He was assaulted, overcome by forces outside his understanding. One moment all sense of position and direction was gone. A moment later he was at the top of the upper cliff looking out over a distant landscape beneath. His hand reached out over woodland, fields and valleys, and he knew he could have them in his grasp to crush or enjoy at will. The next second it was gone. He was back at the foot of the upper cliff with the demon eyes above him, shocked, drained and numb. He saw again that fearful clarity with its sense of implacable loss, but he knew it now for what it was – a vision of the world devoid of soul; mechanistic and barren; survival without life; stark, material and particular. A hard fury burned inside him. He cried out against the numbness of spirit that the removal of his pain brought with it.

He knew that removing his cancer was a mere ploy to gain control of him. He wanted to shout out that he would not be used, but he could not. Fear of the cancer's return checked him and the words died in his throat. What if he just did nothing? What this demon was offering him was no more than it had offered Hérault. Hérault had made the bargain long before he first came to the monastery – survival and the choice of power – and had failed, but he need not make Hérault's mistakes: all he had to do was to do nothing. The disease was gone and he could simply make his way down through the woodland back to normality. Tim was probably dead by now, anyway.

But at the thought of Tim, the rage hardened inside him again. The fiend that menaced him from above had shown it could destroy him in a moment, but Frank had moved beyond the fear of that as though a ratchet had clicked another notch from which there was no going back.

'You brought all this about! You corrupted Hérault and destroyed the monastery. You turned him into a hollow creature possessed by you. Tim is dead or dying because of you! And now Hérault is out of your grasp, you want me!'

'You fool! Hérault came willingly to me for what I could offer him. Everything he did was empowered by me. That was the bargain. He played and he lost. He lost because, given one thing to do on his own, he failed. Learn your lesson well and you'll not fail!'

'I will take no lessons from you!'

'You have already! Why do you think Hérault shot Tim? Because you had already abandoned him. Having made your choice, Scanlon, you sacrificed him yourself. You brought him to me, and abandoned him to me!'

Frank felt he was about to be sick. His legs, which had jarred with pain when he was thrust back onto the cliff top, still flamed with the agony of his burns. He locked his knees rigidly like a wooden doll to stop them from buckling. He would not kneel before this creature. It was true. At the moment the demon-call had raised the spectre of the old monastery walls he had known that both Hérault and Anselm had indeed survived through the centuries – and if they could, why not he? He did not know what had brought it about, but at that moment he had rejected Tim for whatever could offer him that same chance, and within minutes he had seen Tim shot down.

He looked frantically around. What could he do? What weapon had he against this creature? As he looked away from it he lost its focus. The bat-winged, inhuman shape he saw when he looked at it dissipated into rocky shadows when he looked away, but there was no help there: the demon-call dragged him back to the dark reality like a scrap of debris in a whirlpool. The pain in his legs screamed at him, competing with the demon for his attention. Rigidly he held them straight.

He would not kneel. If he knelt before this creature he would be sucked in. How could he defeat it?

'Frank!

He heard his name, then once again, 'Frank!'

Just that, no more, but it felt like a ship's anchor in a storm. He had always treated his name formally. Tim was one of the few people who called him by his Christian name without him feeling self-conscious. If he was honest he preferred it that way, probably because of his youthful dislike of the shortening of his name from Francis to Frank, yet Mary had changed all that. Frank had suddenly become a name to be proud of. More than that, it had a purpose, a lance thrown in battle. And this was a battle.

All he was, all he could be, was somehow there in his name, holding him together. And here he was, Frank Scanlon, standing in pain, rigid, refusing to kneel to a devil. He who had never knelt to anyone in his life. It could almost be laughable. What was the point of it all? Whether he stood on a patch of grass or knelt on it, what benefit was that to anyone?

The point was that to kneel was subjection. He had been told that this creature was also a child of God, but one fallen '*deep and far away*'. To kneel to it was to put himself beneath that depth. Was that the answer? To kneel before God was to acknowledge the Absolute. Before this thing it would be self-destruction. The ground shook and the turf rippled as though he stood on a marsh.

He was not a praying man – not even a particularly religious one. Although a sense of God had increasingly pervaded all these events it had not once occurred to him to pray. Even coming face to face with Mary Magdalene had not changed this. He had already come to terms with the confusions of time and place, and she was so evidently and practically present that there had been no sense of religiosity in meeting and talking with her. His only sense of the spiritual had been negative, in the sense of loss in the demonic view of the world.

The earth shook under his feet again. The creature's eyes coruscated in its black surface like dull fires. Were they really eyes? Frank was reminded of the fall of Hérault into the dark stone. He peered and recoiled. For a moment he had stared into the pit of hell on whose black depths terrifying images swirled and were gone, each instantly replaced by another. The sound shrieking in his ears was despair. The crawling fires that were the eyes of hell were not fire at all. Oh God, what had he seen? Again the word *God* seemed to echo in his mind like the toll of a deep bell. For the first time he felt the appalling significance of the words, 'He descended into hell,' and closed his own eyes against it. Perhaps for the first time since his childhood, he truly prayed.

\* \* \*

Tim sat in the Sanctuary, supported by Anselm and Mary. He was conscious and aware of his weakness. Images swam before him like a delirium. The relics on the table seemed to dance before his eyes. The fractured neck of the jar gaped like the mouth of a tomb. The towel shifted and moved. He was dimly aware that it moved because it was tied around the waist of a man he knew and who was kneeling at his feet. Frank was there – no, he was somewhere else but Tim could see him. He called out. 'Frank!'

Frank did not appear to respond but stood rigidly, staring upwards.

'Frank!'

Tim saw him tremble as though he would fall and tried to raise a hand to support him, but he was too weak and Frank seemed far away, teetering on rigid legs, holding out his arms to someone Tim could not see. It was getting darker. The Sanctuary lamps appeared dim and Tim recognised his increasing weakness. He knew he was losing blood fast but needed to hold on for Frank's sake. He had never been afraid of death for himself but could be fiercely protective of others. Frank was battling with something Tim could not understand. The lamps dimmed further and the darkness of the walls began to close in. He tried to see the Namestone on the reliquary table but disconcerting shadows got in the way.

A voice full of guttural sounds promised healing and life – no, not life: survival. That was the word Frank had used earlier: 'There is survival here.' Something had been seriously wrong then, and it was now, but Tim could not pin it down. Another voice offered life and healing but Frank was struggling between the two. He was visibly trembling, so much so that Tim fancied he felt the tremors in his own body. The lanterns flickered in sympathy with the struggle, and images of the ruined slopes competed with those of the old monastery which Tim saw for the first time, only for it to fade into that of the trees at the edge of the wood.

From the trees he could see Frank more clearly, standing at the foot of the upper cliff, some twenty feet from the Sanctuary entrance, at a spot where the wall had tumbled over the lower cliff and left a gap. His arms were still held out as though pleading, while he maintained his unnatural stiff-legged stance. It took Tim some seconds to realise that his friend's rigid posture was the result of an extreme effort to prevent himself from falling. The trees spoiled his view, but when he tried to reach out to part the branches he was surprised to find his hand clasped. The trees faded and he found himself still in the Sanctuary between Anselm and Mary. The man kneeling before him had taken his outstretched hand in his own. His other hand stroked its way up Tim's arm. Tim felt the gentle warmth of it as it gripped his shoulder; then firmly and with increasing pressure it felt down his back to the wound. The warmth increased and became a searing pain that burned deep inside him. 'Go.'

The pain faded, and with it went the feeling of weakness and loss of blood. He felt stronger – stronger perhaps than he had ever felt, and he had always been a fit man.

The man's eyes held his. Tim saw in them the reflected lanterns of the Sanctuary and then in them again the images of the trees of the wood. 'Go.'

He could not see Anselm now, nor Mary, just the other with the towel that he knew better than either of them. The lamps faded into light seen dimly through leaves. His face felt wet with the sting of rain in the wind. Ahead of him on the sloping outcrop, Frank continued his dialogue with someone or something Tim could not see.

Frank pleaded with the God that he had acknowledged until this moment as no more than a backdrop to what he would have called 'real life'; merely God. Now that real life had been pulled out from under him he had nowhere else to go. The ground continued to shake under his feet and a wind stripped leaves and twigs from the woodland and flung them at him, cutting and stinging at his burns. Small stones skittered from the cliff-face and fell about him, their spatter getting in his eyes.

'God!' Frank shouted. His face stung from the assault of the elements and debris. Try as he would, he could feel no reply. 'God! God!' His words whipped away in the wind. Before and above him the demon shape clung to the cliffs, its harsh discord driving through him.

There was a moment's respite in the wind, then a crash of lightning and instantaneous thunder such as he had never heard before. He thought he must have been struck but he still stood, dazzled by the intensity of the flash so that he saw nothing but the after-image of the illumined cliff with a black shape in the centre that even the lightning could not lighten.

Still he stood and his vision slowly returned, that malevolence still clinging above him, beating its howl of command on him like a weapon. The earth beneath his feet rang with the combined echoes of thunder and discord. A great blast of air almost threw him off his feet. Where in all this was God – if there was a God? He began to fear that this chaos was all there was – a fury of wind, storm and earth-shaking malevolence. Just that and himself, Tim, Anselm, Mary and the creature before him. Could creatures exist without a creator? Was it all madness? And yet they did exist, and in some form or another continued to do so. Sustained by what? One another? They seemed to need one another, even the gross negation on the cliff before him had used Hérault, as it was trying to use him.

Mary's words echoed in Frank's mind: 'Existence must always be coexistence. The recognition of this is the beginnings of love.' If that is the beginnings of love, what is its fulfilment? What is the totality of coexistence? Complete oneness with the beloved? He had never found it easy to obey the religious instruction to love God. He could neither see nor hear Him. As far as he could tell his belief was rational, understood perhaps, and arising from the way the world is, but one cannot rationalise love and so he had found it hard to love God. Now before him he saw the complete antithesis of love, so other that even though it sought to master him and he had spoken with it, it was like conversing with some dangerous force of nature. Like Hérault, but more so, it had cold, plausible rationality without love. Frank recalled again that flawed sense of clarity with which he had seen the world, sharp and defined but with its spirit etched away. He turned away.

Where was the Sanctuary? For a moment he had lost his bearings. The demonic howl increased behind him, almost to a physical assault, but he no longer felt drawn by it. He still failed to locate the Sanctuary but it did not seem to matter. He could hear the name-sound, a still small voice. It was not an alternative to the discord. The discord was an infinitesimal part of it, not separate but 'fallen deep and far away', still a part of the echoes of all times and all places, the song of the stones of the children of God, the One Song of the Word made flesh and of all loves, one Love. He realised that the discord could not be separate from all this and continue to exist. Existence is coexistence. Like Hérault, it could only find absolute independence in oblivion. Was it its failure to realise this that made it demonic? Or its desire to draw others into its own destruction?

He did not need to enter the Sanctuary. He knew now that he was in it all the time, 'in all places and at all times'. The song pervaded everything, and everything shone with its light, and the light was the light of GOD. It condensed before him into the bright shining substance of his own Namestone. He reached out and took it.

'God is good; His love endures forever!'

\* \* \*

The man kneeling at Tim's feet reached out and took his hand. The image of the trees at the woodland edge returned. Tim closed his hand around branches and found himself leaning back against a trunk.

'God is good; His love endures forever!' the voices of Anselm, Mary and Frank merged in his ears with a host of others. He looked across to where Frank had been standing but saw little for the heavy rain. He raised himself to his feet and was surprised to find himself more than strong enough. With a rush of wind, the clouds and rain cleared, and he made out a huge black shadow on the upper cliff. The ground below where Frank had been standing was bare but illuminated by a light, like that of the Sanctuary lamps. There was a crash of lightning and thunder like the wail of the damned, and the shadow split into a vast crack. Slowly the whole cliff face moved outwards. Smoke or spray billowed from it and the whole mass fell onto the ruinous slope beneath. Boulders cracked and burst, a splintering crackle, sparks flying from the striking of stone on stone. There was a moment's pause during which the ground under Tim's feet groaned and shook, then the whole floor of the monastery ruins collapsed downwards as its supporting cliff gave way, creating a downdraught of wind. Through the cloud of dust and rubble, for an instant that stayed in Tim's mind long afterwards, Frank still stood, untouched in the glow of the Sanctuary lamps. Then everything vanished in a pall of dust. When it settled, Tim looked out from the woodland at a new cliff edge just twenty yards away. Frank was gone and, down below, the bodies of Fenster and Harpin lay buried under a million tons of rock and rubble.

Tim felt the aftershocks trembling in the earth for what seemed to be several minutes but was actually about ten seconds. The site of the Sanctuary was gone forever, but somewhere its lamps still burned, and Tim knew that he and Frank were under its protection.

There was sadness at their separation, certainly, but not despair. A fine rain, trailing one of the last clouds, stopped almost as soon as it began. He removed his damp jacket and examined the stained hole, finding it curious that the healing of his wound did not extend to it.

Looking down he saw a smooth rounded pebble at his feet. Something made him pick it up. Perhaps it reminded him of the Namestone. He dropped it into his pocket. It slipped in easily, as stones do, and bumped gently against his side as he made his way to the downward path.

# Epilogue

*I will give him a white stone,*
*with a new name written on the stone*
*which no one knows except him who receives it.*

The Leader's bow is drawn across the universe, calling forth infinite harmonies. From a singularity He draws all creation. Every fundamental particle, every star, every mind is composed in those harmonies.

'Listen! Can you hear your name-sound?

'Look! What do you see?

'What you see, what you hear, has been you from the very beginning. You are far more than the focus of your body and mind. You are focused in the greatest of all minds who has cast aside majesty to be one with you, and less than you, to serve you.'

He who holds eternity in an hour,
To whom a year is as a thousand years,
and a thousand years as a day,
The Logos – the Word of creation
is here in all that is,
even in this single,
very
full
stop
.

# Notes

**Chapter 12:** Hérault quotes from the Rubaiyat of Omar Khayyam[1] leaving out the first two words, 'O love!' which do not fit his purpose.

> Could thou and I with fate conspire
> to grasp this sorry Scheme of Things entire?
> Would we not shatter it to bits
> – and then remould it nearer to the Heart's Desire!

**Chapter 16:** Stephen's Latin prayers were left untranslated to maintain the flow and atmosphere of the narrative. However, for the curious, the English is given below.

*'Sancta Maria, Mater Dei, ora pro nobis peccatoribus, nunc et in hora mortis nostrae…'*
'Holy Mary, Mother of God, pray for us sinners, now, and in the hour of our death …'

*'Deus, refugium nostrum et virtus, populum ad te clamantem propitius respice…'*
'O God our refuge and our strength, graciously receive the people calling to you…'

*'Sante Michael Archangele, defende nos in proelio; contra nequitiam et insidias diaboli esto praesidium. Imperet illi Deus, supplices deprecamur: tuque, Princeps militiae caelestis, Satanam aliosque spiritus malignos, qui ad perditionem animarum pervagantur in mundo, divina virtute in infernum detrude.'*

---

[1] Rubaiyat of Omar Khayyam of Naishapur, Edward Fitzgerald (1809–1883), 2nd edition, verse CVIII (the verse number changes in different editions from 1859 – 1879 and a posthumous edition, 1899).

'St Michael the Archangel, defend us in battle, be our safeguard against the wickedness and snares of the devil. May God rebuke him we humbly pray, and do Thou, O prince of the heavenly host, by the power of God cast into hell Satan and all the evil spirits who roam through the world seeking the ruin of souls.'

*'Misereatur tui omnipotens Deus, et dimissis peccatis tuis, perducat te ad vitam aeternam...'*
'May almighty God have mercy on thee and, having forgiven thee thy sins, bring thee to life everlasting...'

*'Dies irae, dies illa, solvet saeculum in favilla...'*
'That day of wrath, that dreadful day, shall heaven and earth in ashes lay...'

# Background

These notes are intended to help those who feel the puzzling nature of the Namestone (which was intentional) needs enlarging upon.

Written as a time-shift thriller, *Namestone* pits fallible, 'good' people against implacable evil. It is deliberately thought-provoking fiction and deals directly with the inter-connectedness of life and beyond. All errors in the ideas are my own.

It is not a simple 'baddies get their comeuppance' story. The 'villain' makes no excuses or pretence of goodness, or of being misunderstood; rather he makes as effective an argument for being evil as possible to persuade others to his way. *Namestone* deals with the nature of evil and the conflicts it produces in normal people under abnormal stress.

Existence, death and survival are dealt with in a way that touches on what is no more than an iceberg tip of the interplay between age-old faith and a deliberately understated undercurrent of modern Quantum Mechanics. The harmonic trinity of energy, matter and consciousness (or observation) and its counterpoint in the Holy Trinity is one of constant wonder. Nevertheless, it should be read for the thrill and fun of it.

In the story, Hérault is seeking power with complete independence. His goal is unobtainable: the power to feed at will, for example, brings with it dependence on food; the power to go where you will brings dependence on dimension and place. Existence must always be coexistence. The recognition of this is the beginnings of love. Love and hate are opposites, but not opposite poles. They are opposite in the way that existence and non-existence are opposites, light and dark. Love is the complete recognition of oneness with the beloved, the fulfilment of existence and of being. Hate is the absence of this, not something in itself. Ultimately, absolute independence is non-existence.

The Namestone is based on a passage in the book of Revelation:[2] 'To him who overcomes, I will give some of the hidden manna.[3] I will also give him a white stone with a new name written on it, known only to him who receives it.' The white stone mentioned in Revelation had a more mundane source as the customary ticket of entrance to the games in an amphitheatre. The writer of Revelation, however, gave it a greater significance. The Namestone in this story appears grey, not white, to any observer (perhaps other than the owner) because of the infinity of flecks upon its surface. The flecks vary in size – not actually, but as the result of being observed. To a well-attuned observer the particular fleck under observation increases in size to encompass him as a three-dimensional window.

The flecks are ultimately one, not separate. The appearance of discrete points is the result of faulty or ill-understood (non-attuned) observation. The harmony of the name with the stone reflects the harmony of the named 'him who overcomes' with God. It is a reflection of the harmony of the creature with the cosmos, and of the cosmos with God the creator. The name becomes one with the whiteness of the stone, like a spectrum of colours which, when seen as a whole, is pure white. Only the owner of the name can see the totality of the name. Ultimately the stone does not need to be 'present' in its particular form for it to be used. The visible/particular/incarnate form is simply a focus of its much greater existence in harmony with God and all creation.

---

[2] Revelation 2:17 (New International Version).

[3] The hidden manna is linked with many of Jesus' descriptions of himself and his special relationship with our Father, of which the most direct are those found throughout chapter six of John's Gospel: 'the true bread … he who comes down from heaven and gives life to the world … I AM the bread of life …' and numerous others.

Everyone who overcomes the evil in himself is given a namestone, one of many in the whole creation. The eponymous Namestone in the story only has an initial capital as it is specifically associated with Anselm. Ultimately the namestones are one with each other and with God. In the unity of all namestones in God, every named soul remains distinct as harmonies within the greater harmony.

Happy endings and the triumph of good over evil can never be a mere panacea. Sometimes they hide deep down. Sometimes there are greater themes. Hérault's fate is complex. God, being the absolute person, the goal and destination of all true personality, is the antithesis of non-being and of the non-personal. The further one gets from the ground of being and from the One True Person, the less of a person, and the less personality, one can have. The devil ultimately is a non-person, lost like a drop of water in the sea. Far from being the peak of perfection, is the trough of failure. But the grace of God does not let go. It holds on to the last vestiges of the creator in the creature, because his love for the world extends to the lost. There is danger in this. The creature, retaining some personality and ability, can still fight against God and his named ones. That is the risk God takes for us. It is how both Hérault and Simon/Stephen/'Anselm' returned.

The jar is the jar of ointment broken to anoint Jesus' feet by the penitent woman in Luke 7:38 (presumed in this story to be Mary Magdalene – for which there is good evidence). The hairs are those of Mary who used her own hair as a towel and her tears as water for washing. The towel is the towel with which Jesus washed the disciples' feet.

Everyone has his own namestone but it is not given to him unless he has overcome the world and his own carnal nature. Ultimately the namestone is the named one, or, more accurately, every person is an artefact or focus of his own namestone. Possession of one's own namestone is very dangerous. Only those who have overcome the world have the ability to possess their own namestone without being destroyed. Overcoming the world is a spiritual rebirth as a truly spiritual creature, one with the Waters of creation and the Logos and the Name above all names. If one could steal one's own namestone before a spiritual rebirth one would see the flecks of the signature in the stone as one. Not white but black. The creature would behold its own annihilation.

Just as the body is a focus of the stone, so the Namestone is a focus of its greater reality, which is the harmony of the named with the whole cosmos. This is the harmony of all namestones – a network of realities – the soul with God; the cosmos with God; the soul with all souls; all souls with God. Is there a better word than focus? – distillation, essence, representation, image? Image appears to be nearest. Distillation and essence imply that the essence or distillate contains the most important part of the larger thing, whereas the body is just a representation or image of the greater thing.

There is another alternative to Hérault's fate. Just as the Namestone is focus of a greater reality which can be, according to the viewpoint, the sea of souls or the sea of unbeing, so it can also be the focus of the whole cosmos. The cosmos carries in itself the harmonies of all creatures – reborn creatures inhabiting the sea of souls, and the un-reborn, inhabiting the sea of unbeing. The cosmos is therefore the harmony of all creation in the Mind of GOD. A namestone as a distinct focus of a particular creature's harmony is also a distinct focus of the cosmos, and in one aspect a black hole. A creature can thus become lost in a namestone, either by dissemination into the sea of unbeing, or by annihilation in the Ground of Being. The second death?

# Acknowledgements

I would like to thank everyone at Instant Apostle publishers for their help and understanding. In particular Manoj Raithatha and Nigel Freeman, with a very special mention to Nicki Copeland whose sensitive editing skills have gone far to make this book what it is. All errors remaining are my own.

Instant Apostle is a new way of getting ideas flowing, between followers of Jesus, and between those who would like to know more about His Kingdom.

It's not just about books and it's not about a one-way information flow. It's about building a community where ideas are exchanged. Ideas will be expressed at an appropriate length. Some will take the form of books. But in many cases ideas can be expressed more briefly than in a book. Short books, or pamphlets, will be an important part of what we provide. As with pamphlets of old, these are likely to be opinionated, and produced quickly so that the community can discuss them.

Well-known authors are welcome, but we also welcome new writers. We are looking for prophetic voices, authentic and original ideas, produced at any length; quick and relevant, insightful and opinionated. And as the name implies, these will be released very quickly, either as Kindle books or printed texts or both.

Join the community. Get reading, get writing and get discussing!

**instant apⓄstle**